HERE ARE TEN TERRIFYING TALES THAT WILL GIVE YOU CHILLS. . . .

The Halloween Dance

ILLUSTRATED BY JOE RIVERA

The Bad Baby-Sitter

ILLUSTRATED BY VINCE NATALE

Revenge of the Snowman

ILLUSTRATED BY ART SPIEGELMAN

How to Bargain with a Dragon

ILLUSTRATED BY CHARLES BURNS

The Mummy's Dream

ILLUSTRATED BY JOHN JUDE PALENCAR

Are We There Yet?

ILLUSTRATED BY GREG CALL

Take Me with You

ILLUSTRATED BY ROZ CHAST

My Imaginary Friend

ILLUSTRATED BY CLAY PATRICK McBRIDE

Losers

ILLUSTRATED BY PATRICK ARRASMITH

Can You Draw Me?

ILLUSTRATED BY BLEU TURRELL

Also by R.L. STINE

NIGHTMARE HOUR

BEWARE!

Series:

THE NIGHTMARE ROOM

#1 Don't Forget Me!

#2 Locker #13

#3 My Name Is Evil

#4 Liar Liar

#5 Dear Diary, I'm Dead

#6 They Call Me Creature

#7 The Howler

#8 Shadow Girl

#9 Camp Nowhere

#10 Full Moon Halloween

#11 Scare School

#12 Visitors

THE NIGHTMARE ROOM THRILLOGY

#1 Fear Games

#2 What Scares You the Most?

#3 No Survivors

GOOSEBUMPS 2000

GOOSEBUMPS

FEAR STREET

To all the wonderful artists who contributed to this book— your work is haunting at any hour.

For information address HarperCollins Children's Books, a division of HarperCollins Publishers, 1350 Avenue of the Americas, New York, NY 10019.

Library of Congress Cataloging-in-Publication Data
Stine, R. L.
The haunting hour / by R. L. Stine.
p. cm.
Summary: A collection of ten short horror stories featuring a ghoulish Halloween party, a long, mysterious car trip, and a very dangerous imaginary friend. Each story includes drawings by a different illustrator.
Contents: The Halloween dance — The bad baby-sitter — Revenge of the snowman — How to bargain with a dragon — The mummy's dream — Are we there yet? — Take me with you — My imaginary friend — Losers — Can you draw me?
"A Parachute Press book."
ISBN 0-06-623604-5 — ISBN 0-06-623605-3 (lib. bdg.)
ISBN 0-06-441045-5 (pbk.)
1. Horror tales, American. 2. Children's stories, American. [1. Horror stories. 2. Occult—Fiction. 3. Short stories.] I. Title.
PZ7.S86037+ 2001 2001039142
[Fic]—dc21 CIP
AC

First Avon edition, 2002

AVON TRADEMARK REG. U.S. PAT. OFF. AND IN OTHER COUNTRIES,
MARCA REGISTRADA, HECHO EN U.S.A.

Visit us on the World Wide Web!
www.harperchildrens.com

The Haunting Hour

by R.L. STINE

Avon Books
An Imprint of HarperCollins*Publishers*
A Parachute Press Book

Contents

The Haunting Hour

The
Halloween
Dance

INTRODUCTION

I always wanted to be very scary on Halloween. I wanted to be a ghost, or a mummy, or a skeleton. But my parents went shopping and brought home a *duck* costume.

It was white and feathery and had a fuzzy yellow tail. On Halloween night I was embarrassed to go out of the house.

I told my friends I was a *vampire* duck. But they didn't buy that story for a minute. They hooted and laughed and quacked at me all night. It was the worst Halloween of my life.

I remembered that dreadful night when I wrote this story.

It's about two boys who are *dying* to have the scariest Halloween ever. But they quickly change their minds when the thrills turn to chills.

ILLUSTRATED BY JOE RIVERA

I froze in dread—and listened to the words I hoped I'd never hear. "We'll have our own Halloween party at home," Mom said. "Won't that be nice?"

I groaned. My little sister Madison cheered.

"But my friends and I want to go *out* on Halloween!" I protested.

"Mark, you can invite all your friends here," Dad said. "It'll be safer."

Safer? Who wants to be safe on Halloween?

"Invite your whole class," Mom added, smoothing her hand through my hair, which I hated.

Madison cheered again. "Can I invite my whole class too?" she asked, jumping up and down like a monkey.

"Of course," Mom said.

Oh, wonderful.

"We're thirteen!" I said. "My friends don't want to hang out with a bunch of babyish eight-year-olds."

Mom and Dad were always making me do stuff with Madison. They made me take her to the petting zoo. They made me dress up as a clown for her birthday parties. Last Christmas they forced me to sit on Santa's lap with her.

"Stop complaining. It'll be a great party," Mom said. "We'll play a lot of fun games."

"Maybe we'll rent a scary movie," Dad said. He looked at Madison. "Not *too* scary, of course. Just a little scary."

"I'm going to be a little sick," I said.

I'm doomed, I thought. My friends will never speak to me again. I will never live this party down. I'm dead. Dead!

And I was right.

Actually, the party was worse than death.

Only eight or nine of my friends showed up. About thirty of

Madison's friends came, and almost all of them were dressed as princesses!

My best friend, Jake, and I came as hideous ghouls from beyond the grave. Our skin was lumpy and green and decayed, and we had bleeding wounds and deep black scars covering us from head to foot.

I had an eyeball that dangled from its socket and a wad of sick yellow stuff hanging from my nose. Jake had a long brown knife handle sticking out of the back of his ripped, ragged shirt.

I tried to put on some rap music. But the princesses took over the CD player and danced together to wimpy boy-band music. My friends stood around the food table, looking bored.

Mom's babyish games didn't help much. *Pin the vine on the pumpkin?* Whoa. Hot stuff.

Of course, none of my friends joined in. And then when Dad finally pulled out the scary video he had rented, I knew this had to be the worst Halloween party in the history of the world.

Guess what scary movie he picked. *The Wizard of Oz.*

Madison and her friends huddled around the living room to watch. I gave Jake a shove toward the front door. "Come on," I whispered. "Let's go."

He held back. "Huh?"

"Let's get out of here," I said. "I can't take it anymore."

We crept to the door, opened it quickly, and sneaked outside.

It was a cold, frosty night. The front lawn glowed like silver under the rising full moon. The bare trees swayed and creaked.

I watched my breath puff up in front of me. I straightened my ragged ghoul costume and led the way down the gravel driveway.

"Where are we going?" Jake asked, glancing back at the house.

"Anywhere," I muttered. "I don't care. I can't take that babyish party one more minute."

"It *was* pretty disturbing," he said.

My house stands at the bottom of a steep hill. I pointed up the hill. "Maybe there are trick-or-treaters up there," I said. "Why don't we visit some houses and score some candy?"

We started across the street. "Ohh—" I let out a cry—and stopped walking—as a blaring roar exploded in my ears and a white light dazzled me.

The brightest light I had ever seen. Bright and hot, as if the sun had dropped over me.

I raised my arm to shield my eyes. But I couldn't shut it out. My head throbbed in pain.

And then I was blinking in darkness again. The dangling rubber eyeball bounced in front of my face. My ears rang. I squinted at Jake.

He kept blinking too, trying to force away the pain of that strange light. "Did you see that truck?" he cried.

"It—it almost hit us!" I said. "Man, it had to be going a hundred!"

"I thought we were dead meat," Jake said, shaking his head.

I turned and saw someone standing behind us. Another ghoul. A tall, thin kid with a gaping dark wound in the front of his T-shirt.

He had long, stringy hair with fat black bugs poking out of the tangles. One eye was covered with a slimy patch of green gunk.

"Hey—hi," I said, unable to hide my surprise. "Neat costume."

"What's going on?" the kid asked. He had a hoarse, whispery voice, as if he had a cold.

"We've been stuck in a boring party," Jake told him. "We just escaped. You been trick-or-treating?"

"Not yet," the kid said. "My name is Ray. I just got out too." He studied Jake and me for a moment. "Want to go to a *good* party? I mean a *really* good party?"

He didn't wait for us to answer. Limping on one leg, he led the way up the hill. His bug-filled hair blew behind him in the breeze. Humming to himself, he kept glancing back to make sure we were following.

We reached the top of the hill and turned toward the old graveyard on the corner. I was surprised to see no one on the street. No trick-or-treaters. No cars moving. A lot of the houses were already dark.

"Where is this party?" I asked.

"Not far," Ray replied.

Jake and I followed him to the graveyard gate. Tall weeds peeked out between the broken pickets. Beyond the gate the ground sloped up. I could see the crooked rows of gravestones poking up like jagged teeth under the bright moonlight.

"Is—is the party in the graveyard?" Jake asked.

"It starts here," Ray replied mysteriously. He pulled open the gate and waved us in. My shoes sank into the marshy weeds. The air grew colder.

I shivered. "I don't think we're allowed in here," I said. "Are you sure there's a party—"

Ray cut me off by raising a finger to his lips. "Watch," he whispered. His eyes gazed straight ahead at the rows of pale gravestones.

Jake and I stared at the gravestones. I jumped when I heard a *hiss*. It was soft at first, like a whisper.

I lowered my eyes, searching for a cat. But didn't see one.

I heard another whisper across from us. Then more whispers from farther away. The whispers became a steady *hiss*, like steam escaping from a radiator.

I bumped Ray's shoulder. "What's happening?" I asked. "What's making that sound?"

Again he raised his finger to his lips in reply and gazed straight ahead.

The hissing grew louder. It seemed to spread over the ground. And then slender wisps of cloud floated up. Like wriggling snakes, the pale-gray wisps of steam climbed up between the tilted gravestones. The tiny clouds floated low over the ground, then lifted into the air.

"No!" I let out a cry when I saw the first bony hand poke up from the ground.

I saw the fingers unfurl like spider legs. And then the palm of the hand slapped the hard dirt. Then another hand reached up beside it. The two hands pushed, pushed against the earth.

"Unnnnnh." A low groan made me jump.

I gasped when the dirt caved in in front of a gravestone. As the ground split apart, a head poked up from underneath.

I saw tufts of black hair. Then a pale forehead. Then two empty eye sockets in a half-rotted face.

I tugged Jake's arm. "Let's get *out* of here!" I said.

But Jake gazed straight ahead, his eyes bulging, his mouth hanging open. "I—I don't believe this," he whispered. "The walking dead! M-Mark—just like in the movies!"

"But it's not a movie!" I cried. I tried to tug Jake away. But he stood frozen, as if he were hypnotized.

A gravestone tilted and thudded to the ground. A bony woman, with large patches of skull showing through a wisp of gray hair, pulled herself up from her grave. She shook off the dirt, then threw her bald head back in a silent cry.

The graveyard was suddenly crowded now. Ghouls climbed up from their graves, groaning and stretching. Brushing away the dirt, smoothing back the patchy hair on their gray decaying scalps, they staggered over the hard ground.

"The party is over there." Ray pointed to the old caretaker's mansion, dark and abandoned for many years. "Let's go."

"No way," I said, my whole body shaking. "They're dead! Don't you realize? They're dead—and we don't belong here."

"But they won't know," Jake said. "We look just like the dead tonight—don't we? We can sneak in, Mark. We can party with them, and they'll never know. This is *amazing*!"

I stared at my friend. "You really want to do this?"

"Of course he wants to do it," Ray said. "It's Halloween. It's the only night this can happen. And after the party they'll all do the Halloween Dance."

I squinted at him. "What's that?"

He didn't answer.

"Ray—how come you know so much about this?" I asked.

Again he didn't answer.

"Are you coming?" he said instead.

"No," I said. "It's too scary. If they catch us . . ." My voice trailed off as a shiver chilled the back of my neck.

Ahead of us the ghouls were staggering, dragging each other, pulling themselves over the grass toward the caretaker's house, moaning and muttering.

"Come on, Mark." Jake started to tug me. "We'll never get a chance like this. You were complaining about your wimpy Halloween party. Well, here's a party we will never forget!"

"But Jake . . ." I tried to pull free.

"They won't catch us," he insisted. "They won't even know we're here."

I turned to Ray. But he was gone. I saw him up ahead, near the dark mansion, walking quickly toward the front door.

"Let's just stay for a few minutes," Jake said. "We can leave anytime you want. I just want to be able to tell people what it was like."

I didn't want to walk home by myself. And I didn't want to leave my best friend alone here in this graveyard. So I said okay. Then I took a deep breath and followed Jake past the rows of open, empty graves, up the sloping damp grass to the old mansion.

We stopped inside the front door. Candlelight flickered on the cracked walls.

The shadows of the ghouls darted and bent with the light. Shadows danced on the ceiling, on the walls, making it appear as if the whole house had come to life.

Shrill shrieks tore through the frigid air. The eerie figures ducked and bobbed, bending and moving in a strange dance, a dance of silence. No music. But still they moved together, staggering, sliding stiffly in an unheard rhythm.

Jake and I found a place of safety on the front stairs behind a wooden banister. Leaning on the wood rail, we watched the ugly, silent dance.

An eyeless old man groaned as his bony arm broke from his shoulder and clattered to the floor. A toothless woman tore at her hair, her sunken eyes rolling wildly deep in their sockets.

A tall man lifted a short man's head off his shoulders and held it high in a frightening game of keep-away. The short man grabbed frantically for his head. Jumped high for it. Grabbed it and slammed it back into place.

"This is too weird," I whispered to Jake. "Let's go—before we're caught, okay?"

He nodded. "I guess." But his eyes were on the dancing ghouls. Their eerie shadows flickered over the walls as I grabbed his arm and pulled him toward the front door.

"Hello." A girl stopped me. A dead girl. She appeared about my age, except her hair was pure white and her eyes were faded, and the skin on her face was cracked and peeling.

The lace on the old-fashioned collar of her blouse was torn, and she had a long brown stain down one sleeve.

My heart pounded in my chest. I tried to say something, but the words stuck in my throat. I could only gape at her.

"How did you die?" she asked, her voice a dry whisper.

"Huh? Die?" I forced myself to reply.

She nodded.

"Uh . . . it was an accident," I said.

Her eyes sat deep in their sockets, like two shriveled olives. "How old are you?" she whispered.

"Uh . . . how old are *you*?" My voice cracked.

"One hundred twelve," she replied with a strange crinkly smile.

"Me too," I said, swallowing hard. "I—I've got to go now." I turned to Jake. "We have to get away from here," I said through clenched teeth.

But suddenly a hoarse voice from the center of the crowded living room boomed out: *"Let the party begin!"*

Cheers rang out. High peals of laughter.

"Let the party begin!"

I heard shattering glass and turned in time to see a man shove his head through the front window. When he turned back, laughing, he had chunks of jagged glass wedged between his teeth and jammed in his empty eye sockets.

Next I heard a scream, and saw two ghouls leap from the second-floor landing. Flapping their skeletal arms, they fell with a hard crash, bones clattering over the bare floor.

The cheers grew wilder. A laughing skull flew across the living room and bounced off the fireplace wall. Ghouls danced frantically in midair. A headless woman swung upside down from the dark chandelier.

"I—I'm ready to go now," Jake said, pulling my arm. I could see the fear on his face. "Let's leave. Hurry."

Keeping our backs against the wall, we moved through the screaming, laughing, dancing ghouls. We were almost to the door when the party came to a sudden halt.

Everything stopped. Everyone froze in place as if posing for a photo.

Jake and I froze too. What was happening?

I turned and saw the dead girl who had been talking to me. She held a large, square mirror between her bony hands. Light from the flickering candles danced in the glass.

"Will anyone reflect tonight?" she asked softly. "Will anyone reflect?"

Holding the mirror high, she began to walk slowly through the crowded room.

"What is she doing?" Jake whispered. "Why is she carrying that mirror around?"

"Maybe it's some kind of party game," I answered.

The girl held the mirror in front of a pair of ghoulish dancers. From across the room, I could see that the couple made no reflection in the mirror.

The girl moved on to a longhaired ghoul. She raised the mirror in front of him. "Do we all belong tonight?" she asked in a high singsong voice. "Or will someone reflect?"

The longhaired ghoul cast no reflection in the mirror.

I gasped as I realized the dead girl was crossing the room to Jake and me. And suddenly I knew what she was doing.

It wasn't a party game—it was a trap!

Ghouls made no reflection. They were dead. Their bodies didn't appear in the glass.

But a living person—someone who didn't belong at this party—would make a reflection.

Jake and I were about to be caught!

I grabbed the door handle and twisted it. The door wouldn't budge.

The girl raised the mirror in front of us.

"Uh . . . I can explain," I said. "We didn't mean any harm. We'll go now. We—"

I stared into the mirror.

And let out a soft cry of surprise.

No reflection.

I leaned closer to the glass. No reflection.

I brought my face an inch from the mirror. I pressed my nose against the glass.

No reflection. No face staring back at me . . .

Jake's mouth hung open. His eyes bulged as he gaped into the glass. "Wh-where are we?" he said. "Why—?"

The girl turned, swinging the mirror in front of her. She carried it over to a group of ghouls against the back wall.

I felt dazed. The room tilted in front of me. I fell back against the door, gasping for breath. "I—I don't understand," I muttered.

I turned to see Ray standing beside us. Standing so close, I could see that his right cheek was ripped open. I could see his cheekbone poking out.

"Ray—the mirror," I said. "Jake and I had no reflections."

He nodded.

"But why?" Jake asked. "We're not dead. We're *alive!*"

Ray scratched his open cheek. "No, you're not," he said softly. "I saw you—remember? I saw you get hit by that truck."

"NO!" I screamed. "No—you're WRONG!"

"You started across the street," Ray said. "You weren't watching. You didn't see it coming down the hill."

"NO! NO!" I yelled.

"It hit you both," Ray said. "It threw you across the street. You landed right in front of me."

"NO!" I screamed. "NO—YOU'RE LYING! YOU'RE LYING!"

The front door swung open. A blast of cold wind swept in over me. So cold, I thought. From now on, will I feel only cold? Will I never feel warm again?

My whole body shivered. I turned and saw Jake shivering too. His eyes were shut, his teeth chattering.

Someone pushed me, hard, away from the doorway. The ghouls were limping, staggering, groaning, making their way out of the house. The dead girl flashed me her crinkly smile as she floated past.

"Is the party over?" I asked Ray. "Where are they going?"

"It's nearly midnight," he replied, pulling a fat bug from his hair and tossing it to the floor. "It's time to go outside and dance the Halloween Dance."

Ray guided Jake and me outdoors. The full moon floated high in the night sky now. The wind whistled and howled between the crooked gravestones.

"At midnight on Halloween the dead do their dance under the full moon," Ray explained, leading us up the graveyard hill. "For one moment—one terrifying moment—we all freeze. And time stops. Time stands still. And then, when we begin to dance, when our circle moves forward, time moves forward once again."

He sighed. "It's a secret moment. The only time during the year when the living and the dead are one."

Jake and I joined the others at the top of the hill. The wind blew hard, fluttering the ragged, decayed clothes, making the frail, skeletal ghouls shudder and shake.

I heard bones rattle, and the snap of toothless, fleshless jaws. We formed a circle and held hands. Bony, cold hands with icicle fingers.

I'll never feel warm again. The thought kept repeating in my mind.

I gazed up at the moon, the pale, cold moon so high above us now. And I had an idea.

An idea about the Halloween Dance. About time. About the one moment of the year when the living and the dead are together as one.

My eyes darted around the circle of ghouls. Time will freeze, I thought. When we all freeze, time will stop. And when the ghouls start to dance, time will move once again.

Well . . . what if we all dance backward? What if the circle moves counterclockwise? What if we dance to *reverse* time?

Could it work? Could we move time back to *before* the truck accident? Could Jake and I use the Halloween Dance to return us to our lives?

It was a crazy, desperate idea. But I knew I had to try it.

No time to explain to Jake. The ghouls were standing stiffly now, gripping bony, frozen hands, locking into place.

The Dance was about to begin.

Silence fell over the graveyard hill. A deeper silence than I had ever heard or felt.

No one moved. The wind stopped. The grass stood straight and still. Not a sound now . . . not a flicker of a shadow . . . not a creak of a tree . . . not a breath.

Time stopped.

Midnight on Halloween. And time stopped.

We were all alive. And we were all dead.

And then I felt the circle start to move. I heard the *hiss* of motion. The creak of bones. A breath . . . a sigh.

I moved quickly.

The circle started to the left. But I bumped Jake the other way. I lurched to the right. I pulled the ghoul at my side with me.

I took a big step to the right. Would the circle follow?

Yes!

We were all moving now, moving to a silent rhythm. Moving counterclockwise. Backward!

To the right. A step. A step. A step.

And the wind started up again, howling around our strange circle. The trees shifted and creaked. The tall weeds whistled as they whipped low in the wind.

A step. And another. Another.

The Halloween Dance.

The Dance of the Dead. Going in reverse . . .

And I could feel it pulling us back, pulling us back through time.

We were in the abandoned caretaker's mansion.

Step . . . step . . . step . . .

And then we were back down the hill, stopping at the graveyard gate.

Step . . . step . . . step . . .

And then . . . then . . .

Jake and I were standing in the light. The bright, hot light that ended our lives.

Caught in the truck headlights. The light so blinding . . . and now dimming . . . darker . . . darker . . .

Moving back . . . back in time . . .

I knew the Dance was working. I knew that each step was leading us back to our lives.

Round and round I tugged the ghoulish circle. Keep moving. Keep stepping. Got to get back. Got to be alive again!

And then I could see Jake and me at home at the Halloween party. Surrounded by Madison and her princess pals.

Yes! Back home! Back home, warm and alive.

I stopped dancing. I tried to drop the bony hand that held mine. But the ghoul wouldn't let go. He tightened his grip around my fingers. He pulled me along.

Step . . . step . . . step . . .

"Stop," I cried. "Let me go!"

The circle moved faster . . . faster . . . and then . . .

In school. And back at summer camp. And everything moving so quickly now. Step . . . step . . . the ghoulish circle turned again. . . .

Faster . . . faster . . .

In school again. What class was this? What year?

I tried to break free. Tried to break the circle. But the ghoul wouldn't release his icy grip.

"Wait!" I screamed. "Stop! Stop!"

And then on the living-room floor. Isn't that our old house? Before Madison was born and we moved?

Another step . . . the circle finally slowing . . . slowing.

And I opened my mouth and started to cry.

"WAAAAAAAH! WAAAAAAAH!"

Finally, Mommy comes to pick me up. She raises me up over the crib. "What is wrong, Marky?" she asks softly. "Are you well? Do you need to be changed again?"

"WAAAAAAH."

Doesn't she understand? Doesn't she know why I'm crying? The Dance went on too long! Too long!

"What is he crying about?" Daddy says, coming up beside Mommy. He shakes his head and frowns. "What on earth does he have to be unhappy about?"

Mommy raises me close to her face. "Come on, smile, Marky. It's a happy day. It's your first Halloween!"

The Bad
Baby-Sitter

INTRODUCTION

One night when I was a kid, a new baby-sitter came to the house. She was young and pretty, and I looked forward to a fun night.

I was wrong.

As soon as my parents left, the baby-sitter started telling me frightening stories. She told me about a two-headed kid who went to her school. And about a teacher who died but kept right on teaching.

She told me about a scientist who kept a living human brain in a fish tank and brought it to parties. And about a boy my age who had fish gills on his neck and could breathe only underwater.

She told me the stories were all true, and I believed her. By the time I went to bed, I was shaking so hard, I couldn't sleep!

I remembered that baby-sitter when I started this story. And I tried to create a baby-sitter even more frightening than the one I had that night.

ILLUSTRATED BY VINCE NATALE

I was so glad when Mom told Larry and Maryjo they had to leave. And I could see that my sister, Courtney, was glad too. Yes, they live next door, so Mom says we have to be nice to them. Courtney and I try, but *give me a break*.

These kids are oinkers. I'm trying to be polite. But they are total oinkers. *Oink oink*.

In my room that day, Larry found a bag of potato chips I had been saving. You should have seen the way he snuffled down the whole bag—*with the bag shoved over his face!* Then he grinned with the grease shining on his round cheeks and chin.

And the gross burping noises he made. *Come on*—we're twelve years old. Burping hasn't been funny since we were ten.

My dog, Muttley, burst in and sniffed out the potato-chip bag Larry had tossed on the floor. Muttley dove for the bag and started chewing it up.

That big mutt will eat anything. I had to wrestle it from his mouth—and he bit me!

Ha ha. That made Larry laugh.

Later I started to show Larry my new PlayStation racing game. "Give me that, Matthew," he said. He grabbed the controller so hard, he ripped the cord in two.

Did he say he was sorry? No. He started giggling and rolling on his back. Like it was real funny. *Oink oink*.

I could hear my sister arguing with Maryjo down the hall. They fight every time they are together. I don't know what it was about this time, but I heard Courtney shout, "It's not nice to call people names, you moron!"

Sometimes Courtney really loses it when Maryjo is around. She hates Maryjo's scratchy voice and the way she whines all the time. And she hates the way Maryjo is constantly brushing her long blond hair, brushing, brushing—even at the dinner table.

So we were glad when Mom herded everyone together. "Sorry to break up the party, guys," Mom said. "But Larry and Maryjo have to go home now. I'm meeting your dad at the mall. The new baby-sitter will be here any minute."

"Can I have something to drink before I leave?" Larry asked. He always has to have a drink before he goes. Like he'll die of thirst before he gets home.

"Me too," his oinky sister whined.

Mom hurried to get them juice boxes. Then we sent them out into the rain. It was really coming down. I enjoyed slamming the door behind them.

"Oops, it slipped," I told Mom.

Mom squinted at me. "Matthew, that wasn't nice."

"Why do we have to have a baby-sitter?" I asked, changing the subject. "I'm twelve years old. I can take care of myself."

"Your sister is only eight," Mom replied. "Do you really want to be responsible for her?"

I turned to Courtney. She flashed me a devilish grin. Mom was right. Courtney is trouble.

For one thing, she thinks she's a gymnast. She's always doing cartwheels over the couch. Or swinging herself off the banister, trying for a perfect landing.

She likes to climb things too. Like the rain gutters on the side of the house. Last spring she climbed onto the garage roof, and six firemen had to haul her down.

"Courtney doesn't need a baby-sitter," I grumbled. "She needs a *keeper*!"

"Why isn't Mrs. Craven coming?" Courtney asked.

"She's sick," Mom replied. "She's sending someone in her place."

"Thrills and chills." I sighed. "Probably some old lady who will want to play Uno all night."

The doorbell rang. "There she is now," Mom said. "At least give her a chance, Matt."

"Yeah, sure."

I pulled open the front door and was hit by a blast of wind and rain. Staggering back, I stared out at a girl in a purple rain slicker. "I'm Lulu," she said. "Are you Matthew?"

She didn't wait for me to answer. She stepped into the house, dripping pools of water onto the carpet, shaking herself dry like a dog.

"Hi, Lulu," Mom said. "Let me take your wet things."

Lulu handed over her umbrella and rain slicker. Mom hurried to hang them in the closet.

Lulu shook herself again. "It's a shivery night," she said, smiling at Courtney and me. "My favorite kind."

She ruffled her wavy black hair with both hands. I guessed she was fifteen or sixteen. She had round, dark eyes, very pale skin, and bright-purple lipsticked lips, the same color as her rain slicker.

She pushed her hair back behind the shoulders of her black sweater. She wore tight black jeans and shiny black-leather boots. "Hey, guys," she said, "it's nice to meet you both." She had a soft, whispery voice.

Wow! She is a total *babe!* I thought. Awesome!

Maybe a baby-sitter isn't such a bad idea after all!

Lulu sat down on the couch. Muttley came in and nosed around the puddles near the front door. Then, when he didn't find anything to eat, he sniffed Lulu's boots for a while.

"Dogs like me," Lulu said. She reached down to pet the big gray mutt's head. "They know I can read their minds."

She stared hard into Muttley's eyes. "I know what he's thinking now," she said. "He's thinking that he's hungry."

Courtney and I both laughed. "He's always hungry," Courtney said. "He eats everything he sees!"

Mom rushed by, wearing a long raincoat and one of Dad's baseball caps. "See you later," she told us. She turned to Lulu. "Make yourself at home. Don't let them drive you crazy."

"No problem," Lulu said. "I know how to handle them. I'll hypnotize them and put them in a trance."

Mom was already halfway out the door. I don't think she heard what Lulu said. "That's good," Mom called, and the door closed behind her.

I studied Lulu. She was staring deep into Muttley's eyes again. Lulu has a funny sense of humor, I decided.

She clapped her hands together, so hard it startled Muttley. "What shall we do tonight?" she asked. Her dark eyes sparkled in the light.

"Do you like video games?" I asked. "I have PlayStation Two."

"Bor-ring," Courtney groaned. "Can you help me with my cheerleader routine? I'm trying out for the third-grade squad on Monday."

"We don't have cheerleaders at my school," Lulu replied in her whispery voice. "I don't think I could be much help."

"You just have to watch me," Courtney said.

"Yawn yawn," I said.

"Who were those kids I saw leaving your house?" Lulu asked.

"They're not kids—they're pond scum," I replied.

"They live next door, so we have to see them," Courtney said. "But we hate them and they hate us. They're totally horrible."

We told Lulu just how horrible Larry and Maryjo are.

Lulu jumped to her feet. "I have a fantastic idea. Would you like to get even with them?"

I squinted at her. "What do you mean?"

She giggled. "You know. Pay them back for being so gross?"

"Sure!" Courtney and I replied together.

"Then let's bake some mud cookies," Lulu said.

Courtney and I stared at her. "You mean—make cookies out of mud?" Courtney asked.

Lulu nodded. She winked at me.

"Isn't that kind of babyish?" I said. "I'm twelve. I made mud pies when I was three."

"You didn't make mud pies like these," Lulu whispered. A grin spread over her face. "These are very special. And it's a perfect day to make them."

"What do you mean?" I asked. "It's pouring outside."

Lulu's grin grew wider. "Exactly. That's when the mud is *ripe.*"

≈

Courtney and I splashed through the backyard, carrying trowels and a bucket from the garage. I ducked low, but the wind blew cold rain into my face.

"I don't believe we're doing this," I grumbled, pulling up the hood on my rain slicker.

We both squatted in front of Dad's vegetable garden. I held the bucket, and Courtney began shoveling wet mud and plopping it into the bucket.

"Hey—who let Muttley out?" Courtney cried.

The huge dog came racing through the mud and leaped at me. "Hey—down! Get down!" I cried. His big paws smeared my raincoat with wet mud.

"Take the bucket away!" Courtney yelled. "Take it away! He's trying to eat the mud!"

A few minutes later I kicked off my muddy boots and handed the bucket to Lulu. Courtney and I peeled off our filthy rain gear.

Lulu laughed. "I told you to get some mud. I didn't say you should *swim* in it!"

We carried our soaked raincoats to the laundry room. Then we joined Lulu in the kitchen. She pulled out two cookie trays. "Do you have poster paint?" she asked. "We're going to need paint."

Courtney ran to her room and brought back her paint set.

"Okay. Let's get serious," Lulu said.

She dipped her hands into the bucket, pulled out a wet chunk of mud, and slapped it onto a baking tray. "This one is for you, Courtney."

Courtney stared down at the blob of mud. "What do I do?"

"Mold it like clay," Lulu said. "Form it into a person. You know. Like a gingerbread man." A smile spread over her face. "Make it look like Maryjo."

Courtney giggled. "She'll look great in mud!"

"Then I'll do Larry," I said. "I'll give him a fat, piggy snout." Lulu plopped a mound of mud onto my tray, and I went to work.

Using tablespoons and our fingers, we molded the mud to look like our friends. Then Lulu opened the paint jars, and we colored them. Courtney brushed yellow over Maryjo's long hair. I poured red over Larry's face to give him a nice piggy look.

"Now do we bake them?" Courtney asked.

Lulu shook her head. "One more step," she said softly. "You need to add something that belongs to your friends."

"Excuse me?" I stared at her. "Like what?"

"Like a hair or a fingernail clipping or something," Lulu replied. "You have to bake it in the cookie."

"Well, I have *plenty* of Maryjo's hairs," Courtney said, starting to the door. "She brushed her hair with *my* brush today."

"And what about her brother, Larry?" Lulu asked me, squeezing one of my cookie legs into a better shape. "Do you have any of his hairs?"

"No. No hairs." I thought hard. "But that creep spit potato-chip crumbs all over my floor. They're probably still there. Would they be any good?"

Lulu thought for a moment. "They were in his mouth? Yes. Go get them."

My sister and I raced upstairs. I hated to admit it, but making mud cookies of Larry and Maryjo was kind of fun. We hurried back to the kitchen with the hairs and the potato-chip crumbs. Lulu carefully pressed them into the centers of the cookies.

≈

We cleaned up the kitchen while the cookies baked. The odor from the oven was really gross.

But when we pulled the cookies out, they looked great.

Maryjo had a round, lumpy green face and piles of yellow hair. Larry had tiny black eyes and a bright-red pig snout. His blue jeans were big and baggy, just like in real life.

"Good work," Lulu said, clapping her hands. "Very good work."

"What do we do with them now?" I asked.

"You keep them somewhere safe, and then you use them," Lulu answered.

"Huh?" I stared hard at her. "Use them? What do you mean?"

Suddenly the kitchen door swung open and Mom and Dad came rushing in, shaking out their umbrellas. Rainwater rolled off their raincoats. "Wow! What a night!" Dad said. His glasses were completely fogged.

Mom squinted at our cookie trays. "What on earth!"

"We made mud cookies," Lulu told her. "Sort of an arts-and-crafts project to pass the time."

"Ugh. They smell horrible!" Mom said, holding her nose. She turned to Courtney and me. "They're very cute. But do you think you could take them out of the kitchen?"

My sister and I carefully picked up our cookies. Then we said good night to Lulu, who was pulling on her raincoat.

"Remember, hide them away someplace safe," she whispered. "I'll see you again, real soon."

"You're wonderful! I can't believe you got them to do an art project," Mom told Lulu, leading her to the door. "They *hate* art projects."

I carried the Larry cookie up the stairs in both hands. I looked around my room and decided to put it on my dresser top. I'll show it to Larry the next time he's here, I decided. And I'll tell him it looks just like him.

I bumped the cookie against one of the dresser-drawer knobs. "Oh no!" I cried. The right hand broke off and fell to the floor.

I set the cookie down. Then I picked up the little pink hand and tried to press it back onto the arm. But the mud had dried. The hand wouldn't stay on.

Maybe I can Krazy Glue it, I thought.

"Time for bed, guys!" Dad shouted from downstairs.

I dropped the hand onto the dresser top next to the rest of the cookie and forgot about it.

Until the next morning at school.

Larry showed up in class an hour late. When he took his seat next to mine, he shook his head unhappily and held up his right hand.

I gasped when I saw the white plaster cast on it. "Larry—what happened?" I cried.

"Broke my hand," he muttered.

I stared at it. "How?"

He shrugged. "Beats me. I was changing into my pajamas last night, and suddenly my hand felt like it cracked. Dr. Owens couldn't understand it. I've been at his office all morning."

"Did you slam it in a door?" I asked. "Did you bang it on something?"

Larry shook his head. "No. It just broke."

I pictured the broken mud cookie on my dresser and felt a chill run down my back. I couldn't wait to tell Courtney about Larry's hand.

"It's just a coincidence," she said when I met her after school. "That mud cookie had nothing to do with it." She laughed. "Poor Larry. How is he going to eat left-handed? He always uses *both* hands!"

We walked home. It was a sunny, cold day. Fat brown leaves danced around us on the sidewalk. "What if the cookies have powers?" I asked. "What if I broke Larry's hand?"

"No way," Courtney replied. "The cookies are just mud. I'll prove it to you. I'll do something to Maryjo's cookie. Nothing will happen. You'll see."

Courtney and I hurried up to her room. She pulled the Maryjo cookie from its hiding place in the dresser drawer. She set it down on her desk. "Let's see. What should we do to it?" she asked.

She didn't wait for me to answer. She picked up a pair of scissors, and—*snip snip*—cut off all the yellow hair.

I gazed at the cookie with its ragged, bald head. Then I shoved the phone into my sister's hand. "Go ahead. Call her."

Courtney's eyes went wide. "Call Maryjo?"

"Yes. Call her," I insisted. "See if anything happened."

Courtney punched in Maryjo's number. "Hi, Mrs. Rawlins. It's Courtney. Is Maryjo there?" she asked.

Courtney's mouth dropped open. She suddenly turned pale. "Oh. I see," she said. "Well . . . no problem. It wasn't important. Hope Maryjo is okay." She clicked off the phone.

"What? *What?*" I asked.

Courtney slumped onto the edge of her bed. Her voice came out in a whisper. "I—I could hear Maryjo screaming. Her mom said she couldn't come to the phone. She was having some kind of trouble with her hair."

I gulped. "You could hear her screaming?"

Courtney nodded. "She was yelling, 'My hair—it's falling out! Help me! It's all falling out!'"

I stared at the bald cookie on the desk. I suddenly felt sick. My legs were trembling. "We—we have to tell Mom," I said.

I turned and started toward the bedroom doorway. Mom's voice floated up from downstairs. "I'm going, kids. I'm meeting your dad for dinner in town. Lulu is here. Come down and say hi."

Lulu?

Courtney and I both froze. "I'm not going down there," Courtney whispered. "She's too scary. She has powers. She made us do horrible things."

"We have to go down," I said. "We have to tell Lulu the truth. That we don't want to hurt our friends."

"I can hear you up there!" Lulu shouted. "Come down, you two."

Courtney and I made our way down the stairs, clinging to the banister as if it were a life raft. Lulu stood in the living room, arms crossed, waiting for us.

She was dressed in black again, a black sweater pulled down over a short black skirt. A long purple scarf that matched her lipstick was curled around her neck.

"There you are!" she exclaimed, smiling.

"We know the truth about the mud cookies," I blurted out in a trembling voice. "We don't think it's right to hurt people."

A smile spread over Lulu's face. "It's not right—but it sure is fun, isn't it?"

"No," Courtney said. "It's not fun. We're telling. We're telling my parents about it as soon as they get home."

"No, you're not," Lulu replied softly. Her smile faded slowly. "You're not telling anyone. Let me show you why."

She lifted the lid off a square white box beside her on the coffee table. She pulled out two mud cookies and held them up, one in each hand.

Her eyes lit up. "See? I made Matthew and Courtney cookies!"

"Oh no!" I gasped. The Matthew cookie had black hair and a skinny body, just like me. The Courtney cookie was thin and wiry, like Courtney.

"No more talk about telling on me. Let's get busy," Lulu said, holding the cookies in front of her. "We need mud, guys. We're going to bake some more special cookies today."

"No way!" I cried. "You can't force us—"

Lulu plucked a white feather from a couch pillow. A grin spread over her face as she slowly raised the quill of the feather to the Matthew cookie—and plunged it into the center.

"OW!" I screamed, and doubled over with a sharp pain in my stomach. "Lulu—stop!" I gasped.

She twirled the feather in the cookie.

Pain shot through my whole body. I crumpled to the floor. "Please," I whispered. "Please—take it out."

She pulled the feather out of the cookie and, little by little, the pain faded away.

Lulu picked up my sister's cookie. "Do I have to teach you a lesson too?" she asked Courtney.

"No. No. I get it," Courtney said, her voice trembling.

"Then let's get to work," Lulu said. "And do exactly as I say. Unless you'd like to see what happens when I dip your mud cookies in boiling water."

Courtney and I had no choice. I climbed shakily to my feet. My stomach still ached. I couldn't catch my breath.

To my surprise Courtney did a cartwheel. She flipped over to the couch, forcing Lulu to jump back. Then Courtney climbed to her feet and brushed herself off.

"No tricks," Lulu warned. She had the two cookies gripped tightly in her hands. "I like torturing kids." Lulu's mouth broke into a crooked smile. "But I love to torture adults even more! Get moving. Today we will make mud cookies of your parents."

Courtney and I trudged out to the backyard to dig up mud. We squatted by the vegetable garden and started to shovel.

"What was that cartwheel about?" I whispered. "Did you go totally nuts for a moment?"

Courtney glanced back at the kitchen window. Then she dug her hand into her shirt pocket. "Check this out," she whispered.

She held up a long black hair. "I spotted it on the rug. I picked it up when I did my cartwheel."

I began to see my sister's plan. "You're going to use it in a mud cookie?"

Courtney nodded. "Instead of Mom, I'm going to do Lulu."

≈

The plan worked. Courtney and I were a team. My sister made the Lulu cookie. And I kept Lulu busy on the other side of the kitchen. I pretended I had a splinter in my thumb. I made Lulu search and search for it.

Courtney slid the cookies into the oven to bake. When it was time for the cookies to cool, I got Lulu out of the kitchen. I took her upstairs to show her what we had done to the Larry and the Maryjo cookies.

"Nice work," Lulu said, grinning. "You really paid them back for being so disgusting."

When we returned to the kitchen, Courtney's surprise was ready. Lulu stared in horror at the mud cookie on the kitchen counter. It had bright-purple lips, a purple scarf at its throat, and Lulu's long black hair baked into its head.

"NOOOOOOO!" Lulu screamed. "You can't *do* this!" She dove for the cookie.

But Courtney grabbed the cookie out of Lulu's reach.

"Give it! Give it!" Lulu shouted. She made another frantic grab for it.

Courtney tossed the cookie to me. Startled, I caught it in one hand.

And its head fell off.

Lulu screamed again. She grabbed for the cookie with both hands.

Too late. Her head rolled off her neck and bounced onto the kitchen floor.

The head kept right on screaming. Its eyes bulged with horror as it rolled to a stop against the kitchen counter. "Give me that cookie! Give it!" the head screeched.

Lulu's headless body lurched toward me, her arms outstretched. As she staggered forward, the purple scarf unraveled, revealing her open, cut neck.

Clawing the air, she took another step. Another.

Across the room her head screeched and cried, "Give it! Give it!"

Gripping the mud cookie, I backed against the wall.

The headless Lulu, her arms stretched in front of her, her hands grabbing, grabbing, closed in on me.

I was pressed against the wall. My heart thudded in terror.

I tried to duck away from her—and the cookie dropped out of my hand.

It hit the floor. I stared down at it, expecting it to be broken, but it wasn't.

I dodged to the side as Lulu's hands swiped the air in front of me. Now I was trapped. Trapped in the corner.

The headless girl swung her arms again.

Then . . . stopped. She froze.

I gaped in shock as her right shoulder crumbled away and vanished. Then the scarf disappeared. Then her arm crumbled away.

"Hey—Muttley!" I heard my sister's cry from across the room.

I turned and saw the big dog, his head down, his teeth chomping hard.

Muttley was gobbling up the Lulu cookie!

A few seconds later Lulu was gone. Her head too.

Shouting, screaming for joy, Courtney and I threw our arms around Muttley and gave him a hundred hugs. "You're a hero, boy! A real hero!" I cried.

"Thank goodness he eats anything!" Courtney exclaimed.

"We should give him a big steak dinner tonight!" I said. "He's a hero! A hero!" And I hugged him some more.

Courtney climbed to her feet. "Let's get the kitchen cleaned up before Mom and Dad get home," she said.

"No. Leave it," I replied. "Don't touch anything. We need to show it all to them. We have a lot of explaining to do."

"Okay," Courtney agreed. Her eyes searched the kitchen. "Where are the two cookies Lulu brought? The cookies of you and me. Where did Lulu put them?"

"She brought them in here," I said. "And then I think she put them — OH NO!"

Courtney and I began screaming together. "Muttley—no! Drop, boy! Drop! Muttley—DROP! PLEASE—DROP!"

Revenge of the Snowman

INTRODUCTION

I live in New York City. And when you live in such a crowded, noisy place, you overhear a lot of conversations.

One afternoon I was passing a junior high in my neighborhood, and I overheard two boys arguing. "You can be scared to death," a tall boy in a Mets cap said. "It happens a lot."

"No way!" his friend replied. "You can't just see something scary and drop dead."

"Your heart can stop," the first boy insisted. "It can just freeze. You get so scared, you just freeze—forever."

Frozen in fear, I thought, watching the boys run for a bus. Is it possible for someone to be frozen in fear?

And just as I had that thought, it started to snow.

By the time I walked home, the snow was swirling—and my brain was swirling too. I rushed to my computer to write this story.

ILLUSTRATED BY ART SPIEGELMAN

My friend Billy thinks he's real cool. He's always telling us how cool he is—which is only one of the things that annoy us about Billy.

Billy is an annoying dude. Why? I could make a list. . . .

(1) He's stuck-up.

(2) He's a show-off.

(3) He's a loudmouth.

(4) He thinks he's an expert on everything.

(5) He thinks he's smarter and better than us.

By us I mean me—Rick Barker—and my other friends, Loren and Fred. The four of us all live on the same block, and we've hung out since kindergarten.

So we're stuck with Billy, even though we complain about him all the time. I guess our main problem with Billy is that he never stops talking.

And he always talks about *death.*

"Did you know you can tickle a person to death without even touching him?" Billy says.

He's so weird. It's like he's obsessed. He's always telling us disturbing ways people can die.

"Did you know you can itch to death in your sleep?"

"Did you know a tiny feather can kill you if it falls from an airplane?"

Listening to that stuff is not entertaining. I mean, it can mess up your mind—right?

So today the four of us were walking to the neighborhood park, and when we got there, Loren, Fred, and I decided to put one of Billy's wild death facts to the test.

It was a snow day—school had been canceled. And we were in a really good mood.

The snow was at least two feet deep. Some of the drifts came up to my shoulders! It was wild. The whole world looked white. Except for the sky, which was solid blue. A beautiful, cold, crisp day.

Our breath fogged up in front of us as our boots crunched through the thick snow. We thought maybe we could get some little kids to share their sleds in the park.

But what was Billy talking about?

Three guesses.

"Did you know you can be frozen in fear?" he said.

I let out a groan. "Give us a break, Billy."

"No, it's true," he said. "You can be so frightened, your body freezes—forever. You can't talk. You can't move. It's like being scared to death, only you're still alive!"

"Okay, let's try it!" I cried.

I grabbed Billy by the shoulders of his parka. "Let's test this one out!"

I think Loren and Fred and I had the exact same idea at the same time. Billy struggled, kicking and squirming. But the three of us picked him up—and heaved him, feet first, into the tallest snowdrift we could find.

Before he could move, we started packing the snow around him. It was perfect packing snow, wet and heavy.

"Hey! What are you doing?" Billy cried.

"We're turning you into a snowman!" Fred exclaimed.

We worked furiously. Heaving the snow over him. Shoveling heap after heap onto his shoulders, his head.

"Can we talk about this?" Billy screamed. "You know I can't

stand tight places, right? Hey—stop! This is not funny. I'm freezing in here. I'm catching a cold. I can feel it already! Come on! Let me out of here!"

The three of us laughed.

It was pretty funny seeing the guy in such a total panic over a harmless joke.

"It was *your* idea," I said. "Don't you want to test it? Don't you want to see if you really can be frozen in fear?"

"No! No, I don't!" Billy cried.

"Any last words?" Fred asked him.

"Yeah. Get me *out* of here!" he screamed.

Then we covered his head.

We poked some holes near the top for air. Then Loren found two perfect round stones for eyes and a bent twig for a nose. Fred and I scraped and molded the snow to round it off like a real snowman. And we packed it even tighter. Loren finished the job by tying her scarf around the snowman's neck.

"Yo, Billy, how's the weather in there?" I called. "How's it going, big guy?"

He didn't answer.

The three of us stepped back to admire our work.

"Good job!" Loren cried. We slapped high fives with our wet, snowy gloves.

We expected Billy to come bursting out, roaring and flinging snow at us. He could break out easily, I thought. I mean, how hard is it to knock snow away?

But he didn't move.

He just stood there, still as a snowman. The two stone eyes stared out at us.

"Hey, Billy?" I called.

Silence.

"Billy? Hello?"

A long, eerie silence.

"Billy?" I called.

No answer.

Fred laughed. "He's just trying to freak us out." He pulled my arm. "Come on, Rick. There are some kids with sleds on that hill. Let's check 'em out!"

As we jogged over the snow, I glanced back. Billy still hadn't moved. What was he waiting for?

"Hey—American Flyers!" Fred shouted to some little kids. "Can we have a turn?"

≈

How long did we sled? I'm really not sure. The afternoon sun was sinking in the sky. Long blue shadows stretched over the snow. We returned the sleds to the other kids and Loren and Fred went home.

Then I suddenly remembered Billy.

Rubbing my frozen cheeks, I made my way down the hill—and saw the snowman standing just as we'd left it.

Oh, no! I thought. Then I ran up to it and shouted, "Billy? Billy?"

We had forgotten all about him.

My breath caught in my throat. My whole body shuddered.

Was he frozen in there?

It was just a joke. Had we really done something horrible to the kid?

No! Please—no!

I grabbed the snowman's head. "Billy? Hey—answer me! Why don't you answer me?"

The snow was packed tight, like concrete. I dug my gloves in and began frantically pulling it off in big chunks.

"Billy? Can you hear me?"

Flinging snow everywhere, I quickly ripped away the front of the snowman. I clawed the packed snow loose and batted it to the ground.

"Billy? Hey—Billy?"

Furiously, I batted more snow off the round body.

There was no Billy inside.

I staggered back. Where is he? I asked myself, staring at the chunks of snow on the ground. He couldn't have climbed out. The snowman had been standing just as we left it.

A chill shook my body. I pulled my coat tighter but I couldn't stop shivering.

And then I heard a soft whisper from behind me. *"Rick—you froze me. You FROZE me!"*

"No!" I gasped.

I spun around. "Where are you?" I asked, my voice cracking. "I can't see you!"

Silence.

Just the sound of the wind, brushing snow off the tree branches.

Then the whisper again: *"You froze me, Rick."*

And Billy stepped out from behind a tree.

Head down, he moved toward me, lurching, staggering in a strange slow motion.

And then slowly, slowly, he raised his head—and I saw his face. Crusted with ice. Patches of snow clung to his hair and eyebrows. Icicles hung from his cheeks, his chin.

I opened my mouth in a scream of horror.

Billy kept staggering across the snow toward me, his gloved hands outstretched as if ready to grab me. *"Rick, you froze me. You froze me to DEATH!"*

My teeth chattered. Chill after chill ran down my body. I stared at Billy, frozen in fear.

And then I felt something snap.

Something in my brain.

Just a soft *pop*.

I tried to move. I tried to cry out.

But I couldn't.

My legs, my arms—they wouldn't budge. I couldn't open my mouth to scream. I couldn't even blink my eyes!

I stared straight ahead.

Billy came closer. Closer. "Rick—what's your problem?" he asked.

I could see him and I could hear him clearly. But I couldn't answer. Couldn't move my lips or make a sound.

And then I remembered Billy's words . . . *"You can be so frightened, your body freezes—forever."*

"Come on, Rick," Billy said. "The joke is over. I'm okay. Really. Look. The ice and snow—I put it on my face to look scarier. See?"

He pulled a chunk of ice off his cheek.

"Rick— snap out of it," he said. "I'm fine. I waited till you guys left. Then I smashed my way out of the snowman. No big deal. You were busy sledding. You didn't see me break out. You didn't see me rebuild the snowman.

"I put it back together," he said. "Then I hid behind a tree and waited for you to come back."

His hand squeezed my shoulder. I could feel it, but I couldn't move. He waved his hand in front of my face. But I couldn't blink. Couldn't move my eyes.

"Hey, Rick—you're kidding, right?" he asked. "Give me a break. Say something. Did you like my joke? It was good, right? Did I scare you? Come on, Rick—did I scare you?"

How to
Bargain with
a Dragon

INTRODUCTION

A lot of my story ideas start with the question: *What if . . . ?*

This story began with the question: What if dragons were real?

I have always been fascinated by the giant winged creatures. In stories and movies and drawings, dragons have always seemed very real and alive to me. They are fierce and majestic at the same time. Ugly and beautiful. And so much more intelligent than dinosaurs.

I know they are mythical. I know that dragons never existed.

But what if they did?

This is a story about a boy on a terrifying mission. Ned is about to face the fiercest dragon of them all—and he will soon learn the answer to that awesome question.

ILLUSTRATED BY CHARLES BURNS

On a summer day long ago, when birds as big as clouds flew the skies, a boy named Ned journeyed through leafy forests and over green, grassy hills. Ned carried only an apple in his knapsack and a crude, hand-drawn map of the kingdom.

His peasant smock was sweat stained and wrinkled. His long brown hair fell in damp tangles from under the red cap tilted over his suntanned forehead. His brown laced boots were scuffed and scratched, the soles as thin as paper.

As he walked, Ned whistled to keep himself company. The journey was long, and he had no idea of what terrible dangers he faced at journey's end.

As he neared his destination, Ned's legs began to tremble, and chill after chill tightened the back of his neck. His mouth became too dry for whistling. He knew that soon he would be meeting Sir Darkwind, the greatest Dragon Master in the kingdom.

Ned had long dreamed of this day. But now, through the trees, he heard the groans and bleats of the dragons in Sir Darkwind's stable. And Ned wondered which would prove more fierce and menacing—the dragons or the Dragon Master?

He pulled off his cap and mopped his forehead with the sleeve of his smock. "Courage," he murmured to himself. "Be strong and brave. Or you will never reach your goal."

Taking a deep breath, Ned stepped out of the forest and stared at the Dragon Master's house across a field of dirt and stones.

Was it a house or a fortress?

Built of white stone, it rose up like a gleaming mountain in the afternoon sun. Ned saw a narrow door at one end—the only opening. There were no windows!

To the left of the house stretched a tall stone wall at least four times as tall as Ned. Ned gazed in amazement at the faces staring back at him from above the top of the wall.

Broad creature faces on long, scaly, sun-wrinkled necks. Black eyes as big as plums, staring from deep sockets. Ancient, long-toothed faces, craggy and lined with wisdom—and sadness.

Dragons.

Up till now Ned had seen them only in the Sorcerer's ancient books. Gazing at the amazing creatures, Ned remembered the Sorcerer's stories of how the dragons had once moved freely around the kingdom.

"The dragons are a proud and wonderful species," Margolin had said. "They have their own customs, their own habits. Do not be fooled into thinking they are like other animals. Their wisdom is as big as their size. Why are their eyes so sad? Because they have seen *everything*."

Now the old dragons curled their long necks over the stone wall and gazed at Ned in silence. He could hear the heavy *thud* of their feet as they shifted their weight. A pale-yellow dragon on the end coughed, a wet cough from deep in its throat.

Their eyes are not welcoming, Ned thought. They gaze at me as if I'm their next meal. But dragons are not meat eaters—are they?

Ned struggled to remember what the Sorcerer had told him. The old dragon coughed again, spewing yellow liquid over its craggy snout. Another dragon, slender faced with bulging black eyes, let out a long, menacing growl.

Ned took a few timid steps closer to the stone fortress. The dragons tensed as he approached the wall.

And then two dragons shot out their huge heads at him, roaring furiously. The sound was like thunder in his ears. The wall appeared to shake.

With a frightened cry Ned fell onto his back. The dragons' hot breath swept over him. He turned on his stomach and frantically crawled away.

The dragons' heads swung low over the wall, stretching toward him, snapping furiously.

When he was at a safe distance, Ned scrambled to his feet. He brushed the dust off his clothes and straightened his cap.

The dragons stared at him in silence now. Waiting to see if he would approach again.

But Ned kept his distance. The boy cupped his hands around his mouth and shouted, "Sir Darkwind! Sir Darkwind, a humble peasant boy wishes to speak with you."

To Ned's surprise the door creaked open. A dark-robed figure stood half hidden in the doorway. He did not step out.

"What do you want?" he called. He had a high, boyish voice.

"I have come to see the great Dragon Master," Ned said. "To ask a favor."

"I am Gregory, Sir Darkwind's servant," came the reply. "Sir Darkwind does no favors."

Ned swallowed, his mouth as dry as straw. Had he come all this way for nothing?

"I bring the best wishes of the great Sorcerer Margolin," he called. "Perhaps if Sir Darkwind would come outside and give me a moment—"

"We don't know any sorcerers," Gregory sneered. "And Sir Darkwind seldom comes out of his house. Only to whip the dragons to keep them in their place."

Ned squinted at the figure of the servant, still hidden in the shadow of the doorway. "He never leaves his house?"

"No," came the reply. "He has too many enemies."

Behind the stone wall the dragons growled and groaned. A

fierce-looking creature with curled horns on its gnarled head lowered its head and battered the wall.

"Go away! You are upsetting the dragons!" a deep voice bellowed from inside the house.

Ned saw another figure move into the doorway, shoving the servant aside. Even from a distance Ned could see that this man was tall and wide, his white robe billowing around him.

The sight of him sent shivers down Ned's back. It was known far and wide that Sir Darkwind was the cruelest man in the kingdom. Even the Sorcerer Margolin, with all his powerful magic, had feared him.

"Are you the great Dragon Master?" Ned asked. He dropped to his knees and bowed his head. "I am a humble peasant boy, grand sir. I come to beg for work."

"You want to work for me, boy?" Sir Darkwind roared. "What do you know about these beasts?"

They are not beasts, Ned thought. Yes, they are fierce creatures. But they have the wisdom of the ages. Even I know that.

But he did not correct the Dragon Master. Instead, he said, "I am a fast learner, sir. I need work badly. I have five brothers and sisters, and my family is poor. My father's foot was crushed under a wagon wheel. Now they all depend on me for their bread."

"Tsk tsk," the Dragon Master replied sarcastically. "Am I supposed to cry for your ill fortune?"

Dragons grunted and growled. High clouds rolled over the sun. Inside the house Sir Darkwind appeared to go deeper into shadow.

"Have you worked before, boy?" the Dragon Master asked.

"Yes, Sir Darkwind. I was apprenticed to the Sorcerer Margolin," Ned replied, still on his knees. "But I was forced to leave that job. After Margolin had a terrible argument with another sorcerer, they both suddenly vanished."

"Good riddance," Sir Darkwind said. "The world doesn't need sorcerers. A good strong *whip* is the only magic I need!"

Ned climbed to his feet, brushing dirt off the hem of his smock. "It would be an honor to work for you, Sir Darkwind. Everyone knows you are the greatest Dragon Master in the world!"

A sharp laugh escaped Sir Darkwind, more like the bark of a dog. "I am the *only* Dragon Master!" he bellowed from the darkness of his doorway. "These are the last dragons to survive. The last in the world."

"I would be honored to help tend to them," Ned offered.

Sir Darkwind laughed again. "You would swing the whip to help teach them their manners?"

"No, sir. But—"

"What then would you do?" the Dragon Master shouted. "What is your bargain? All of life is a bargain. That is the one truth that I have learned. So what is your bargain, boy? What bargain do you wish to make with me?"

Ned stared openmouthed into the dark doorway. "I have no answer," he said finally. "I offer myself as a humble worker."

He saw Gregory, the black-robed servant, return to the doorway. He and the Dragon Master had a hushed conversation. As they talked, the clouds rolled away from the sun. Behind the wall several dragons raised their heads to the sunlight.

"Come a bit closer, boy," Sir Darkwind ordered. "I have a bargain for you."

Ned took a few steps toward the house. He still couldn't see the man clearly. He could see only the wide expanse of his white robe.

"There is one dragon still roaming free," Sir Darkwind announced. "One dragon not in my collection. And I want them all!

All! Here is the bargain I will make with you. Bring the last free dragon to me, and I will make you my apprentice."

Ned uttered a startled gasp. "Capture a dragon?" he cried. "But how? It will breathe fire on me, and I will perish."

From inside the house Gregory laughed.

"Fool! Dragons don't breathe fire," Sir Darkwind boomed. "That is a fairy tale."

"But—I have no weapon to use against a mighty dragon!" Ned cried.

"And I have none to give you. You must use your wits, boy," the Dragon Master said.

"How did you capture all these dragons?" Ned asked, pointing to the fierce creatures watching from the stone wall.

"I made a simple bargain with them," Sir Darkwind replied. "I told them if they came to stay here, I wouldn't kill them and use their meat for dragon stew."

Some bargain, Ned thought.

"Listen to me carefully, boy," the Dragon Master called from the darkness of his doorway. "The last free dragon is called Ulrick. It lives in a cave on top of Stone Hill. If you capture this dragon and bring it to me, my collection will be complete. I will give you a job so that your family can eat."

"But—but—" Ned sputtered.

Sir Darkwind disappeared into his house. The door slammed hard.

Behind the wall the dragons all began to shriek. Several of them snapped their jaws at Ned. A very young one, still green and slender, raised its head and uttered a high wail that sounded like crying.

≈

The afternoon sun was high in the sky as Ned began to walk back through the forest. Waves of heat rose up from the ground, making the trees appear to bend and shimmer.

Stone Hill, a steep-sloped mountain of smooth gray rock, led to a high cliff. Ned knew that deep caves were cut into the sides of the hill.

No one ever explored those caves. People were afraid of the fierce creatures that lived inside.

What weapon can I use to battle a dragon? Ned asked himself. The dragon will have talons a foot long and teeth the size of tree stumps. How can I make a bargain with a dragon like that?

The sun beat down on him, making him feel as if he were melting. He stopped in the shadow of tall ferns to catch his breath.

He thought of the cruelty of the Dragon Master. How he whipped the old dragons. How he kept them prisoners in that walled pen.

Imagine, thought Ned, having so many enemies that he cannot leave his house!

After several hours' walking, Ned reached the bottom of Stone Hill. He mopped his forehead with his sleeve and took a deep breath.

He could see black holes all along the side of the smooth rock hill. He shuddered, wondering what kinds of creatures made their homes in those caves.

He leaned forward, lowered his head, and began to climb. His boots slid on the smooth stone. He kept his arms stretched out at his sides to keep his balance.

Halfway up the steep slope his leg muscles began to cramp. With a troubled sigh Ned slipped into the dark opening of a cave. He dropped to the dusty cave floor and rubbed his aching leg muscles.

Despite the heat of the day, the cave felt cool and damp. Ned leaned his head against the wall and shut his eyes.

I have been walking for two days. Perhaps a short nap will refresh me, he thought. Then I shall continue my journey to the top.

He didn't sleep long. A shrill whistling awoke him. It sounded like a thousand flies droning in his ear.

Ned's eyes shot open—and he let out a cry.

Giant albino cave rats!

They had dragged a goat into the cave and were eating it alive!

The goat kicked and squealed. But the rats swarmed over it—dozens of them. They held it down with their fat, white-furred bodies and buried their fangs in its belly, ripping away chunk after chunk of red flesh.

I'm next! Ned thought. As soon as they discover me . . .

Too late to run. Whistling and chattering, the cave rats turned from the now-silent goat—and scurried around Ned.

They were as big as dogs, with long fangs still dripping with goat blood. They had round red eyes that glowed like burning embers.

Their fat pink tails slapped the stone cave floor, beating a terrifying rhythm of attack. The circle tightened, and the ugly creatures began to shriek as they closed in on Ned.

"Eeeeeeeeee eeeeeeeee!"

Their shrill cries sliced through Ned's head, so loud he covered both ears.

And jumped to his feet.

The albino rats were as tall as his waist! Their snapping jaws competed with the *thumpthumpthumpthump* of their battering tails.

"I'LL MAKE YOU A BARGAIN!" Ned yelled.

Startled by his shout, the rats stopped their shrieks. The glowing red eyes burned like fires against the blackness of the cave.

"Here is my bargain," Ned announced. "If you give me half a

chance, I'll run away and never come back!"

He didn't give them time to decide. He jammed his hands onto the tops of the heads of the two nearest cave rats—and leapfrogged over them.

Then he took off, racing out of the cave and up the steep, rocky side of Stone Hill. From below came the albino rats' shrieking and whistling. But he knew the rats wouldn't chase after him. They couldn't survive in sunlight for long.

By the time Ned reached the top of the hill, his heart was thudding and his legs felt heavy as lead. The sun was a red ball sinking behind the hill, giving everything a rosy glow.

Ned struggled to catch his breath. He gazed at the cave opening in front of him. It rose like a giant triangle. Enormous bones, dry and bleached white by the sun, were strewn at the entrance.

Those are too big to be human bones, Ned told himself. But the ugly sight made his chest feel fluttery and his stomach lurch.

"Oh!" Ned cried out as a low grunt echoed from the cave. He heard rumbling footsteps. Another grunt. A sour odor floated out and washed over him. Holding his breath, he took a step back.

The dragon is in there, he knew. He suddenly realized his whole body was shaking.

A bellowing roar from deep in the cave made the stones shake beneath the peasant boy's feet. I have no choice, he told himself. I have to go through with this. But I am terrified. Will I be able to speak?

He sucked in a long, deep breath. The air tasted foul and damp.

"Ulrick!" he called. "Ulrick—my name is Ned, and I have come to see you!"

He didn't have to wait long. He heard another grunt. And then more heavy, plodding footsteps. The ground shook again, and the cave appeared to explode, as a giant brown creature burst out and rose over Ned. A dragon bigger and more fierce than any in Sir Darkwind's collection.

Its roar made the tree limbs shake. The dragon snapped its jaws, revealing rows of jagged yellow teeth. It clicked its long talons as if preparing to pounce.

Leathery wings flapped furiously on its back. Its huge round eyes gaped at Ned like two cold, dark suns. As it lowered its massive head over him, hot yellow drool splashed from its open maw and sizzled on the ground.

It—it's going to swallow me! Ned realized. He dropped to the ground, trying to shield himself with both hands.

The dragon lowered its huge head . . . lower . . . lower . . . until Ned felt its burning hot breath on the back of his neck.

Then the creature opened its jaws wide, wide enough to swallow Ned whole.

"WHAT DO YOU WANT?" the dragon bellowed.

Ned dropped flat on his back, nearly smothered by the creature's hot breath. "You—you talk?" he choked out.

"Of course!" Ulrick boomed. The dragon's round eyes flashed like solid black marbles, reflecting nothing. "All dragons speak when there is something to say!"

The boy and the dragon held a long staring match. Finally Ned's terror faded enough for him to stand and find his voice.

"Ulrick, why do you stay by yourself up here?" he asked. "Are you not lonely? Why don't you join the other dragons down below?"

The dragon tossed back its head and roared. It arched its leathery back and raised sharp talons as if ready to attack. Again, it lowered its head inches from Ned's.

"Live with the Dragon Master?" Ulrick bellowed. "Do you know *anything* about the Dragon Master, Ned?"

Ned swallowed hard—and waited for the pain of having his head bitten off. He opened his mouth to reply, but no sound came out.

"All my brothers and sisters used to roam free, in peace," Ulrick boomed. "We are no threat to humans. We do not hunt for animal flesh. We eat only the Gorsel bushes and the red berries that grow on them."

Ulrick bumped Ned's shoulder with its snout. "Do you know how the great Dragon Master captured all his dragons?"

Ned rubbed his shoulder. "Uh . . . no."

"HE DESTROYED ALL THE GORSEL BUSHES EXCEPT HIS OWN!" Ulrick bellowed. "The dragons had a choice—starve or be captured. As soon as the dragons followed him home, Sir Darkwind clipped their wings. He whips them and keeps them penned up. He charges a fee to see them. And he forces the dragons to roar and battle each other for the crowds."

Ulrick's chest heaved up and down. In a roar of fury the dragon snapped open its jaws.

The wave of hot breath sent Ned onto his back once again. He stared up helplessly as, wings flapping, the mighty dragon roared and raged.

"And now you want to capture ME and add ME to Sir Darkwind's sad collection?" it boomed. "NEVER! NEVER!"

A shadow swept over Ned. The shadow of the dragon's giant head.

"Noooo!" Ned let out a scream as the jaws closed around him. The pointed teeth dug into Ned's chest and back.

And then the dragon lifted him, lifted him easily off the ground.

Ned thrashed and squirmed like a worm caught in a bird's beak.

The dragon tilted its head back to swallow him.

"NO! WAIT!" Ned wailed. "WAIT! NO! PLEASE! NO! NOOOOOO!"

≈

The next morning the servant Gregory arose early and went out to check on the dragons. The sun, still low over the trees, hadn't burned through the morning fog.

Gregory carried the water bucket to the trough where the dragons drank. Around the pen the dragons groaned and stretched sleepily.

Staring into the damp gray mist, Gregory let out a startled cry. The water bucket fell from his hands. "D-dragon!" he exclaimed.

Was it just a shadow in the fog?

No. An enormous dragon was lumbering toward Sir Darkwind's house, swinging its head from side to side, wings fluttering on its back.

In his excitement Gregory tripped over the water bucket as he ran to the house. "Sir Darkwind! Sir Darkwind!" he shouted. "A dragon approaches!"

The Dragon Master was just finishing his breakfast. He jumped up from the table, egg running down his bearded chin, and hurried to the door. Squinting into the fog, he clapped his hands joyfully.

"It is Ulrick!" he declared. "My collection is complete. Ulrick is coming to join the others."

"But where is the boy?" Gregory asked. "The boy is nowhere to be seen."

The Dragon Master peered out from the doorway. "You are right, Gregory. The dragon comes alone." He tossed his head back in a cruel laugh. "Ulrick probably had the boy for breakfast!"

"But then why has the dragon come here?" Gregory asked.

"Go see," Sir Darkwind said. He gave Gregory a hard push out the door. "Go see at once—while I wait in the safety of the house."

His legs trembling, his heart fluttering in his chest, Gregory obeyed his master. He stepped up to the dragon, took a deep breath, and shouted up to it: "Ulrick—the Dragon Master demands to know: Why have you come?"

Ulrick gazed down at the trembling servant. The dragon's eyes were cold and blank, like two black rocks. It snorted loudly, a sound that made Gregory quiver all the more.

In the pen beside the house all the other dragons had lined up. They stood very still, watching the newcomer.

Gregory glanced back and saw the Dragon Master waving his hands impatiently.

"Sir Darkwind desires to know why you have come," the servant repeated, unable to stop his voice from cracking with fear.

With a sudden motion the huge dragon swung down its head and almost bumped Gregory to the ground. Gregory gasped and leaped back.

And then slowly, very slowly, the dragon opened its massive jaws.

"Oh nooooo," Gregory moaned. He saw the boy's head inside the dragon's mouth. The head, eyes shut, rested on the creature's fat red tongue.

"You have eaten him!" the servant shouted. "You have eaten the boy!"

Gregory couldn't bear the awful sight. He spun around wildly. "Sir Darkwind! Horrors! Horrors! The dragon—it—it . . ."

"What is it?" the Dragon Master called from the house. "What are you trying to say?"

"The d-dragon—" Gregory stammered. "Sir Darkwind! Sir Darkwind! You must come and see this! You must come at once!" And then he fainted to the ground in a heap.

What must I see? Sir Darkwind wondered. Why is the dragon standing there with its mouth open like that?

The Dragon Master cautiously stepped out of the house. As he strode up to the dragon, the dragon turned and opened its jaws wider.

And Sir Darkwind saw the boy's head, resting so comfortably on the fat tongue.

He saw the boy's dark hair matted wetly to his forehead. And saw the boy's peacefully shut eyes.

Sir Darkwind scowled up at the dragon. "Did you think that would shock me? You have wasted your time, Ulrick!"

"I do not think so," Ned said, opening his eyes. "I *knew* this would get you out of the house!"

He freed his arms from the dragon's throat, then grabbed hold of the massive teeth and pulled himself out. Lowering himself to the ground, he brushed back his hair and wiped dragon drool off the front of his smock.

Sir Darkwind's eyes bulged in surprise. "How—how have you done this, boy?"

"I made a bargain with the dragon," Ned said. "Just as you instructed me."

The Dragon Master's face filled with confusion. "And now the dragon is mine?" he asked.

"Not quite," Ned replied. "That isn't the bargain."

He rubbed his hands dry on the side of his smock. "You see, before the Sorcerer Margolin disappeared, he taught me many of his spells," Ned said. "And now I'm going to show you one of my favorites."

Ned waved his hands, mumbled several strange-sounding words—and the Dragon Master began to change.

His body appeared to melt. His face sank into his body. Leafy limbs sprouted all around him. And bright-red berries popped out around the leaves.

Ned mumbled a few more words. And then he smiled. The spell had worked. He had turned Sir Darkwind into a Gorsel bush.

The dragons all roared happily. Tears the size of raindrops, tears of joy, poured from their ancient eyes.

"My mission was to destroy the Dragon Master and free the dragons," Ned said. "But first I had to trick him into leaving the house! As you can see, I have succeeded."

"You have kept your bargain with me," Ulrick said. It gazed down at the Gorsel bush. "How long will your spell last?"

"I don't know," Ned replied. "It doesn't really matter—does it?"

"No. Not really," Ulrick replied.

And then Ulrick bent its head low and began to devour the bush and its tasty berries.

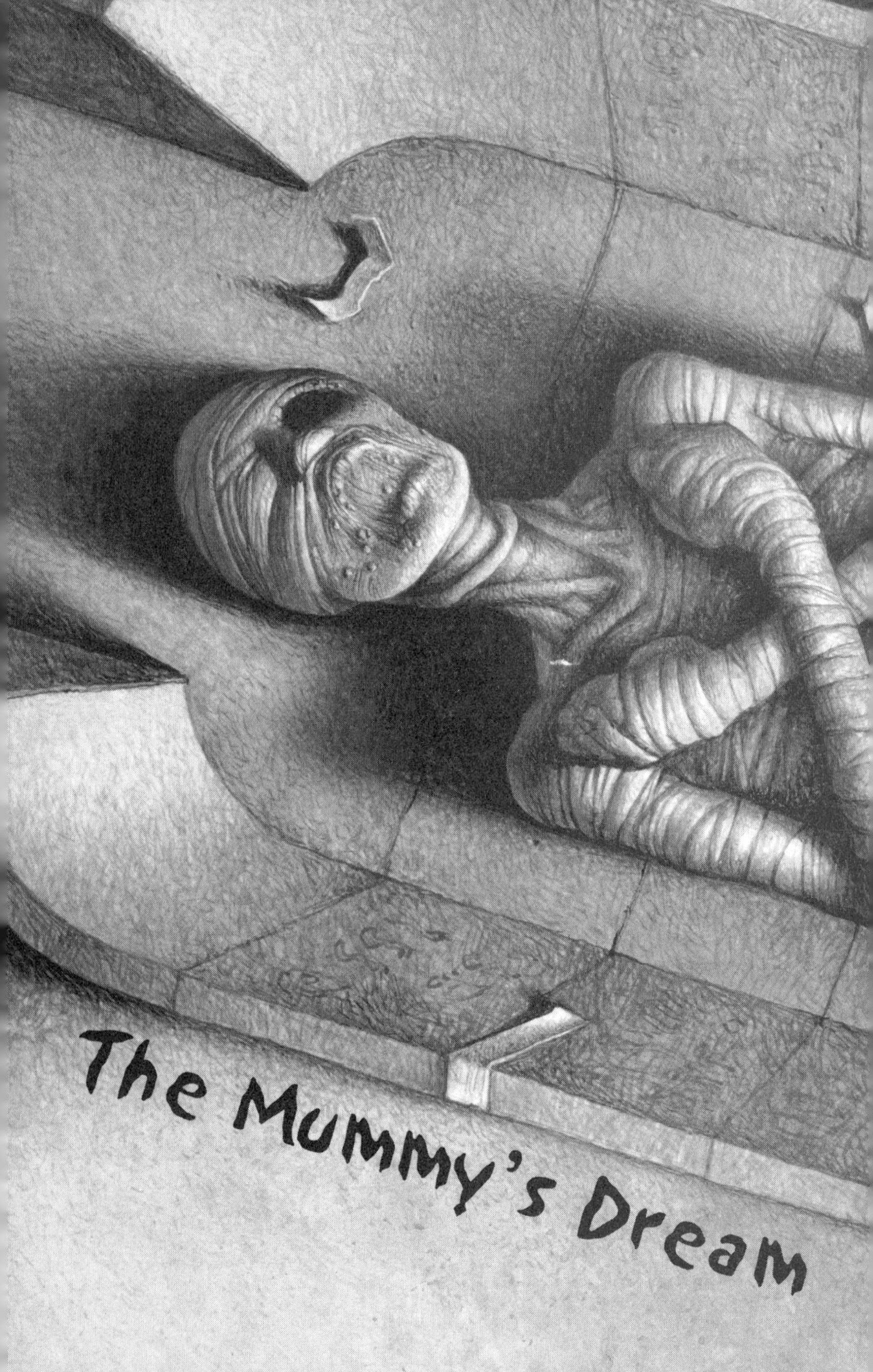
The Mummy's Dream

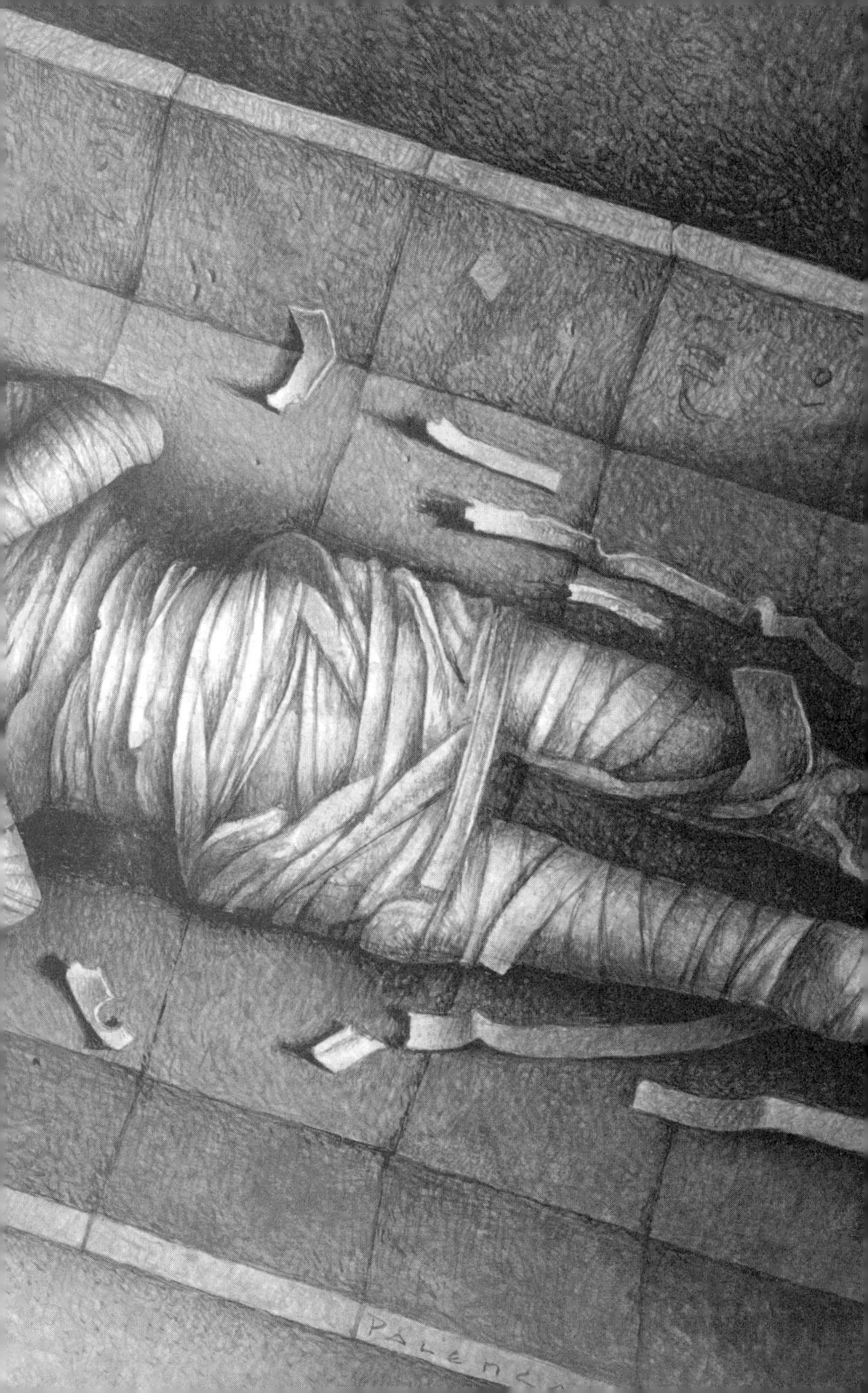

INTRODUCTION

The museum in my hometown was very small. When we visited there on school trips, my friends and I always headed to the same place—the mummy room.

I'd lean over the big stone case and stare down at the ancient mummy. He seemed to stare back at me through the layers of gauze and tar. His arms were crossed over his slender chest. The gauze wrapped around his body was stained and torn.

One day our fourth-grade class visited the museum. I headed straight for the mummy room. I was staring down at the ancient figure when a few of my friends decided to be funny.

As I leaned over the case, they grabbed me. They lifted me off the floor—and started to drop me headfirst into the case.

I let out a scream. I didn't want to fall on top of that mummy. I didn't want to touch him.

Luckily my friends saw a guard approaching. They quickly pulled me out and stood me on my feet.

Ever since that close call, I've always wondered what it would be like to lie on the bottom of a cold, ancient mummy case.

This is a story about a boy who finds out.

ILLUSTRATED BY JOHN JUDE PALENCAR

I gazed over Joanna Levin's shoulder into the glass display case. A small sign above the case read: ANCIENT EGYPTIAN ART. Bracelets and necklaces and long golden earrings gleamed under the bright lights.

"Wow. They're incredible!" Joanna declared. She poked her finger against the glass. "I want that one and that one."

I shook my head. "They're from four thousand years ago, Joanna. They probably cost millions."

Joanna shoved me away. "It's *my* birthday," she said. "Why can't I pick out a few presents?"

"It's not a gift shop. It's a museum," I replied.

She shoved me again. "Connor, you're about as much fun as a toothache."

"This is a cool party, Joanna!" Abbey Foreman called from across the room.

"What a great idea," Debra said. "Having your birthday party at the science museum."

"And we have the whole museum to ourselves," Joanna said.

My friend Josh tugged my arm. "Check it out, Connor. The mummy room. Over there."

Josh and I made our way to the next room, our shoes clicking on the hard tile floors.

The mummy room was small and dimly lit. It had a low green ceiling, which made the room seem even darker.

Photographs of the pyramids in Egypt hung on one wall. In front of the photos stood a pile of crumbling yellow bricks. A sign said they were actual stones from King Tut's burial tomb.

Two big stone mummy cases sat a few feet apart in the middle of the room. The cases were open, their stone lids propped against the wall opposite the photos.

Josh and I ran up to the first case. It was tall and deep. We had to stand on tiptoe to see into it.

I leaned on the case and peered down. The smooth stone felt cold on my hands. "Empty," I said.

"It looks like a huge bathtub," Josh said. "Do you believe that a dead person actually was in here?"

Joanna and the other kids gathered around the other case. "Oh, gross," Debra Fair groaned, making a disgusted face.

Josh and I squeezed in next to her and gazed down at the mummy. Its head and body were completely wrapped with gauze. The gauze was stained and torn in spots. You could see the black tar underneath.

One eye had become uncovered. The empty eye socket was filled with tar.

"Yuck," Joanna said. "Do you think there are millions of bugs crawling around inside it?"

"Bugs can't get in," I told her. "The bodies were completely emptied. Then they were covered in hot tar before they were wrapped. They were wrapped too tightly for anything to get in. And the coffin lids were sealed tight. No way bugs could get in."

Joanna frowned at me. "Connor, how come you know so much about mummies?"

I shrugged. "I just do."

Rising on tiptoe, I turned back to the ancient mummy. His arms were crossed tightly over his chest. He seemed to stare up at me with that one tarry eye.

"Do you know how they got the brains out of his head?" I asked Joanna. "They used a long tool to go up into the skull. Then they pulled the brain out through his nose."

"Ohhh, sick," Joanna groaned.

"Shut up, Connor!" Abbey cried.

Josh and I laughed.

"Let's get out of here," Joanna said, hurrying to the door. "Let's go look at the sphinx."

The others turned away from the mummy case and followed her to the next room. Their voices echoed off the tile walls.

Josh and I stayed behind. We both studied the mummy for a while.

"I wonder how old he was when he died," I said. "People didn't live very long back then. Most of them died in their twenties."

"Maybe he was just a kid," Josh said. "Wait! What's in there?" He pointed to a half-open door in the corner.

I followed him over to it and peeked inside. "It's just a supply closet," I said.

"But check this out, Connor." Josh bent into the closet and pulled out a ball of something. "Strips of cloth," he said. He started to pull it apart.

"They probably use it for dusting," I said.

"But it looks a lot like mummy gauze," Josh replied. "There's piles and piles of it in there." He laughed. "Enough to make our own mummy."

I stared at Josh. Josh stared back at me.

"Are you thinking what I'm thinking?" I asked.

He was.

We had to work fast. It was a simple plan. Josh wrapped me up in the cloth until I looked like a mummy. Then I climbed into the empty mummy case. I crossed my arms over my chest and stretched out.

"Quick. Go get Joanna," I said. The layer of cloth muffled my voice. "Hurry, Josh. It's hard to breathe."

Josh peered down at me. I could barely see him through the gauze. "After I bring Joanna and the others, you sit up very very slowly, okay? And whisper Joanna's name."

"Got it," I said.

"She'll jump out of her skin!" Josh exclaimed.

"Just hurry . . ." I begged. "My face itches, and I can't scratch. And it's hot in here."

He disappeared. I settled against the stone case bottom. I tried to relax, but I was really uncomfortable.

The stone was hard. And I was already sweating.

I shut my eyes and counted to ten.

Where are they? What is taking so long?

Finally I heard voices. I sucked in a deep breath and held it. It would spoil the joke if someone saw me breathing.

Poor Joanna, I thought. In a few seconds I'm going to scare her to death!

The voices came closer. I could hear them right above me.

My heart started to race. Time to do my mummy act, I told myself.

Slowly, very slowly, I raised my head and began to sit up. *"Joanna . . ."* I whispered.

I waited for the screams.

Instead, I heard a man's voice. "Prince Akor, there you are."

"Huh?" I gasped. I sat up straight.

"We have been searching for you," the man said.

"Whoa. I'm s-sorry?" I stammered. He's a museum guard, I thought. He's caught me in this valuable mummy case. I'm in major trouble.

I fumbled with the strips of cloth and managed to tug the cloth away from my eyes. "I—I'm really sorry," I started. "It was just a joke. I—"

I gasped as I saw the men standing around the mummy case.

They were short and thin and very tanned. Their heads were shaved bald.

They wore knee-length white robes that looked a lot like girls' dresses. And leather sandals with straps that went all the way up their legs.

I frantically tore away strips of cloth. "Who . . . are you?" I asked.

And as I stared at them in shock, I realized that the room had changed. The dark, tiled museum walls were gone, as was the low green ceiling. These walls were made of bright-yellow brick that seemed to reach up to the sky. The room was enormous!

The other mummy case had vanished. Flaming torches hung on the walls. A giant golden statue of an owl towered over the doorway.

My mind was spinning. "This . . . this is unreal," I whispered.

An older man in a long white gown reached out a tiny tanned hand to help me from the case. He had bright-blue eyes and a tight smile. Wrapped around his head was a white-and-blue headdress that hung down over the sides of his face to his shoulders.

"Prince Akor," he said. "So this is where you are hiding. We have been searching for you since the sun's first light."

"Prince *what?*" I cried. "There is a big mix-up here. I'm—I'm not a prince." My voice came out high and shrill. I was so frightened, so stunned and confused, I didn't sound like me at all.

His smile faded. Those bright-blue eyes burned into mine. "Fear not," the man said. "You are in my hands, Prince Akor. As you have always been."

"But—but—you don't understand!" I sputtered. "I don't know how I got here. I—"

"We all know why you were hiding here," the man said, nodding solemnly. He placed his hands on my shoulders and squeezed them.

"We cast no blame for your terror."

"My—*what?*" I cried out again.

The man turned to the others. I counted six of them, all tanned and bald, all standing stiffly in their white robes. "Priests, take the prince to the altar," he ordered.

They all bowed their heads in unison. "Yes, High Priest," they said.

"No. Wait!" I shouted. "It's a mistake! I—I've got to find Joanna and the other kids."

I took off. I didn't know who these men were. I just knew I had to get away.

I started for the door, but the men surrounded me. They formed a tight wedge and forced me to move with them. The High Priest led the way.

"You're making a big mistake!" I shouted. "I'm not who you think I am!"

We walked through a long, wide tunnel lighted by torches all along the wall. The tunnel seemed endless. My legs shook so hard, I could barely walk. My brain spun with questions.

How did this happen? I asked myself. This looks like ancient Egypt. But how can that be? Who is Prince Akor? Where are these men taking me?

The tunnel led to a big chamber that reminded me of a church. The altar at one end was covered with tall candles. Black cats stalked everywhere. A large golden sun hung across from the altar.

"All bow to Ra, the God of Sunlight," the High Priest ordered. The priests all bowed, murmuring strange words to themselves.

The High Priest stepped forward and took my hand. "I am sorry for your fear, Prince Akor. But it will not last long."

I opened my mouth to speak, but only a squeak came out. My

heart was beating too hard for me to talk!

The High Priest led me away from the altar. We crossed to the other end of the vast chamber.

"Oh no," I said when I saw what stretched across the back of the room. An enormous square pit of bubbling tar.

"We have all heard of the plot against your life," the High Priest said, lowering his voice to a whisper. "Your enemies plan to murder you—and leave your body unmummified. These evil ones plan to rob you of your afterlife!"

I stared at him. My mouth dropped open. His words weren't making any sense to me.

Was he saying that someone planned to kill the Prince? And not turn him into a mummy?

I knew that the ancient Egyptians believed in life after death. And I knew they believed that a body had to be mummified in order to have a life after death. But what did all that have to do with me?

"Fear not," the High Priest said, taking my hand again. "I have taken care of you since childhood, my Prince. I shall not allow these enemies of Egypt to rob you of your afterlife. I will mummify you *today*!"

"No!" I finally found my voice. I finally understood what he was saying.

"Listen to me!" I screamed. "You've got it all wrong!"

The six priests all gasped in shock. The High Priest took a step back.

"You're trying to kill the wrong guy!" I told them. "I'm not your Prince Akor. My name is Connor Franklin. And I don't come from here. I'm from Cincinnati, Ohio."

The men started to mutter. The High Priest waved to them to stop. He frowned at me, his blue eyes studying me hard.

"I live in the United States!" I cried. "In the twenty-first century! This is all some kind of crazy mix-up."

By the time I finished, I was gasping for breath, my chest heaving up and down. I waited for the High Priest to speak.

"You have had these dreams before, Prince Akor," he said softly. The priests all nodded.

The High Priest reached forward and began to unwind the strips of cloth that still covered me. I gasped when I saw what I was wearing underneath. Not my jeans and T-shirt. A short white skirt!

"This is crazy!" I cried. "I don't come from here. I come from far in the future!"

"If that is true, how do you understand us?" the High Priest asked, speaking softly and patiently. "How do you speak our language?"

Good question.

I stared at him openmouthed. I didn't have an answer.

"You have dreamed before that you lived in a future time," the High Priest said. "But you must realize that you are awake now. The dream is ended."

He placed his hand tenderly on my shoulder. "I promised your father, the Pharaoh, that I would always take care of you. And I will keep that promise. I will mummify you before the night falls."

My whole body shuddered. "No, please. Listen to me!" I begged.

"Of course you are afraid, my Prince," the High Priest said. "But you will be given a potion to dull your senses. You will not feel the burn of the hot tar. When the ceremony is over, you will be lost to Egypt. But you shall live forever with the gods in the afterworld."

A low cry escaped my throat.

No thanks, I thought. I'm outta here! As soon as someone turns his back, I'm outta here!

"Priests, take him to rest in his chamber while I prepare the tools," the High Priest commanded.

Once again the six men surrounded me and forced me to walk with them. They led me to a large chamber filled with brightly colored cushions. Hanging from the high ceiling, silky blue curtains fluttered in a gentle breeze.

"Rest, Prince Akor," one of the priests said, bowing his head. "We will come for you soon."

The heavy door closed hard behind them.

I realized I didn't have a second to waste.

I ran to the door and tried it. Bolted shut.

I turned and saw the long curtains swaying gently. There is a breeze, I realized, so there must be a window.

Yes! Hidden behind the curtains was a small window, shaped like a triangle, high on the yellow stone wall.

I scrambled over the cushions to the wall. The window was over my head. But I grabbed the sill with both hands and pulled myself up.

I looked outside. In the far distance a red sun was setting over low hills of yellow sand. I stared down to a brick courtyard far below. It was a steep drop straight down. Nothing to break my fall.

It was a tight fit, and the window was tiny. But I had no choice. I had to try it. It was my only chance to keep my brain from being pulled out of my nose and my body from being wrapped in hot tar and gauze.

Huddled on the narrow sill, I swung my legs out the window. Then I slowly pushed my head out . . . my chest . . . my arms.

I took a deep breath—and jumped, landing hard on my feet.

"Ow." Pain shot up from both ankles. My legs folded. I fell to the pavement.

Get up! I ordered myself. No time to waste.

Ignoring the pain, I climbed to my feet. I searched the courtyard. No one here. But I knew that the High Priest would soon be sending all of his men after me.

My eyes scanned the wall of the building. It seemed to stretch forever. Was that a doorway down near the far end?

I took off, running despite the pain that throbbed from my ankles. I needed someplace to hide, someplace where I could think. Where I could try to figure out my next move.

I ducked into the darkness of the open doorway. I blinked hard, waiting for my eyes to adjust to the dim light.

I saw torches on the walls. And then, in their darting light, I saw the mummy case.

I was back in the chamber where they had found me. I took a deep breath and held it, trying to slow my racing heart. The mummy case glowed dully in the dancing torchlight.

Suddenly I had an idea. A desperate idea. But an idea.

My sweaty hands slipped on the stone as I hoisted myself into the mummy case. Quickly I stretched out on my back and crossed my hands over my chest.

The High Priest said I've had dreams before, I thought.

But *this* is the dream. This isn't real. I'm dreaming *now*.

I'm dreaming that I'm in ancient Egypt. I'm dreaming that I'm a Prince who is about to be mummified.

If I can fall asleep, I can dream myself back. I can wake up back in Cincinnati where I belong. If I can fall asleep, I can get myself back to Joanna's birthday party.

I shut my eyes. The stone case felt cool on my hot body. I tried to force myself to relax.

"Please—let me wake up in that mummy case in the science museum," I begged out loud. "Please—let me wake up in the twenty-first century. Let me wake up in that mummy case. . . ."

I forced myself to breathe slowly . . . slowly . . .

I tried to clear my mind.

Darkness washed over me. A soothing, calm darkness.

I don't know how long I slept. But as I awakened, I heard voices.

I gazed up and saw a low green ceiling over my head.

Yes!

I'm back, I realized. I wished myself back to the twenty-first century. What a horrifying dream I had!

I felt so happy, I wanted to jump up and dance around the museum.

But for some reason I couldn't move.

Why can't I move? I wondered.

The voices came closer. They were right above me now.

Kids poked their heads over the mummy case. They gazed down at me.

Who *are* those kids? I don't know them. Where are my friends?

"*Ooh,* gross," a boy said, shrinking back from me.

"Sick," a girl beside him groaned. "Look at the putrid stains. He's all decayed."

Wait. Why are they saying that? I thought.

"Bet he has worms crawling in him," a boy said.

"That's disgusting."

The faces disappeared. I stared up at the ceiling, thinking hard.

And I knew what had happened. It took me a while, but I figured it out.

Yes, I was back in Cincinnati. Yes, I was in the mummy case in the science museum.

"NO!" I wanted to scream. "No! It can't be! It *can't* be! I'M THE MUMMY!"

Are We There Yet?

INTRODUCTION

For our summer vacations, my parents used to take us on long car trips. My brother and sister and I were squeezed in the backseat—and we'd argue and fight the whole way.

As we rode, my mom would point out every cow and horse. My dad *always* got lost. We *hated* these trips! They always ended with the three of us kids screaming, "Let us out of this car!"

"No problem," my mom would shoot back. "This is a one-way trip. You don't have to ride back with us." She meant it as a joke. But I always wondered—what if she was serious?

ILLUSTRATED BY GREG CALL

My brother, Artie, and I did not want to go on a long car trip with my parents. We were unhappy, and we didn't keep it a secret.

"Are we there yet?" Artie whined, hunched beside me in the backseat.

Mom laughed. "Artie—we just backed down the driveway!"

"But when are we going to get there?" he asked.

"We'll get there when we get there," Dad said, slowing for a stop sign. Dad likes to talk in mysteries.

I don't *like* mysteries. I like to get to the point. "Why are we taking this stupid car trip?" I groaned.

"For a vacation," Mom said.

"But we always go to the beach for our vacation," I said.

"Not this year," Dad said, his eyes straight ahead on the road.

Beside me, Artie had settled back against the seat and was punching away at the Game Boy he held in his lap. "Richie Corwin went on a car trip with his parents last week," Artie said.

"Did he enjoy it?" Mom asked.

Artie shrugged. "I don't know. He didn't come back yet."

We passed several cars as Dad slid into the center lane of the highway. "Pam and Kelly went on car trips this summer too," I said.

"See, Tammi? It's the cool thing to do!" Mom said.

"Did either of them come back yet?" Dad asked.

Something about the way he asked that question made me pause. His voice sounded so strange—kind of tight.

"No. Not yet," I said.

≈

"Where are we?" I asked. "We've been driving for hours, and there's nothing out there but farms and flat fields."

"It's a big country," Dad said.

I grabbed the back of Mom's seat and leaned forward. "Come on. Give me a hint where we're going. Just a hint." I reached for the road map spread out on Mom's lap. "Let me see where we are."

"Here." Mom picked up the map and did her usual comedy act with it. Unfolding it. Turning it from side to side. Crumpling it up. Uncrumpling it. Turning it upside down and inside out.

Dad started to laugh. He loves Mom's comedy acts.

I finally got fed up, tried to pull the wrinkled map from her hands—and ripped it in half!

That made Mom and Dad *roar* with laughter.

"We have two maps now," Dad said. "So we must be in two places at once!"

That didn't make any sense at all.

"We've driven right off the map!" Mom exclaimed.

More laughter.

But the laughter stopped when Artie opened his mouth in a horrified scream. "Stop the car! *Dad, stop the car!*"

Dad hit the brakes hard. The tires squealed as the car slid, swerving onto the tall grass beside the highway.

I grabbed the door handle, swung it up, and pushed open the door.

"What on earth is this about?" I heard Mom cry.

But I was already out the door, running through the grass, chasing after the dog Artie and I had spotted out of the car window.

"Here, boy—come! Don't be afraid!" Artie called.

The big dog stopped at the edge of the highway. A truck roared past, blowing the dog's yellow-white fur up on its back.

"I think it's a collie," I said breathlessly, catching up to it.

"Is it a stray?" Artie asked. "Do you think someone let it loose on the highway?"

I glanced back and saw Mom and Dad standing beside the open car doors, watching us, hands on their hips.

"Good dog! Good dog!" Artie called softly, bending down.

The big collie's thick fur was all tangled. It lowered its head, nuzzled Artie's hand, and began to lick it. I petted the dog's back.

Dogs love Artie and me, and we love dogs.

Mom says we have a special relationship with dogs because we're almost as smart as they are. That's supposed to be a joke.

But Artie and I take dogs very seriously. They are wonderful, loving animals. And they need people like Artie and me to take care of them.

This wasn't the first time my brother and I had made Dad stop the car because we saw a dog running loose on the road. Once we saw a cute little terrier get run over by a van. We had nightmares about that for weeks. I never forgot the terrible squeal the dog let out when the tires rolled over its back.

I brushed back the collie's fur and searched for a collar. No. No collar or ID tags or anything.

The collie had the biggest brown eyes I had ever seen. "Who would let a beauty like this loose?" I said, rubbing its ears.

Cars whirred past. Artie and I carefully led the dog away from the highway.

"Not again," Dad sighed when we reached the car. "Do we have to return him to his owner?"

"We can't," I said. "No tag. He'll have to come with us."

"No room!" Mom exclaimed. "One of you will have to run alongside the car!"

"I will!" Artie volunteered, raising his hand.

A blue pickup truck bounced up onto the grass and came to a stop behind our car. A young man with long, stringy hair and a thick stubble of beard stuck his head out of the driver's window.

"Hey, Fletch!" he shouted, waving at the dog. "Fletch—get back in here! Bad dog!"

The collie burst out of Artie's hands, flew over the tall grass, its tail wagging furiously, and eagerly leaped into the back of the truck.

The young man turned to us. "Thanks!" he called, flashing us a thumbs-up. "That dog is always trying to give me a scare."

He gunned the engine, and the truck skidded back onto the highway as Artie and I waved good-bye.

≈

We stopped for dinner at a restaurant called The Barbecue Barn. Artie and I were starving. We were putting away the barbecued chicken and mashed potatoes. I glanced up and noticed that Mom and Dad still had full plates.

"We're just not very hungry," Mom said.

They were both quiet too, I realized. Artie and I kept trying to guess where we were going. "Just give us a hint!" we begged. But they wouldn't play along.

They kept glancing at each other. Once I saw Dad squeeze Mom's hand under the table. He let it go when he saw me watching.

"What's wrong with you two?" I asked.

Dad shrugged. "Nothing. Tired from the long drive."

"Have some of those collard greens," Mom urged. "We don't have those back home."

Artie stared down at the pile of greens on his plate and made a face. "Yuck. It looks disgusting."

"Go ahead. Taste it," Dad said. "You have to be brave."

"Yes. Brave," Mom repeated. And suddenly, I saw that she had tears running down her cheeks. "You both have to be brave."

"Mom? What's wrong?" I asked.

But she spun away, wiping the tears off her face.

I turned to Dad. He shrugged. "Finish your dinner," he said. "We've got miles to go before we stop for the night."

After dinner, we drove west, into the setting sun. Red sunlight covered our windshield. Then suddenly, we were rolling through a heavy, dreamlike darkness.

I must have fallen asleep. I let out a sharp cry as a hard bump shook me awake. Dad had turned into a gravel driveway. I glimpsed a red-and-green neon sign blinking in the dark. It was supposed to read: WAYSIDE MOTEL. But the L was burned out, so that it read: WAYSIDE MOTE.

Squinting out the window, I could see a long, low building and a row of doors and dark windows. The only window with some light behind it had a sign that read OFFICE.

Dad stopped the car in front of the office. Artie leaned forward, suddenly wide-awake. "Is this where we're staying tonight? Do you think they have a video game room?"

Mom yawned. "Too late for video games," she said softly. "It's been a long day. You'll be asleep in five minutes."

Artie and I had our own room. Mom was right. We were so exhausted from riding all day, we climbed under the thin blankets and fell right asleep.

The next morning, cold gray light seeped in through the dusty window. I woke up, blinked, trying to remember where I was. I stretched. My back ached from the hard bed.

I squinted at my watch. Past nine o'clock.

Weird, I thought. That's really late. Mom and Dad like to get an early start. Why didn't they wake us up?

I shook Artie awake. He blinked at me. "What's up?"

"We slept late," I said. "Let's go find Mom and Dad."

Yawning, we stepped out into the cool, gray morning. Mom and Dad's room was next to ours. I knocked on their door—and it swung in. Had they forgotten to lock it?

"Mom? Dad?" I called.

No answer. Artie pushed the door open all the way, and I followed him in. "Hey!" I let out a startled cry.

The room was empty. The bed was made.

"Wrong room," Artie said.

We stepped back outside. I felt a cold raindrop on my forehead. Then another one on my hair. We moved to the room on the other side of ours. I knocked on the door. "Mom? Dad?"

No one in that room either.

I stared down the long row of motel rooms. Which room were Mom and Dad in? "We'd better ask at the office," I said.

We turned and started jogging toward the office. Artie stopped suddenly—and pointed to the gravel parking lot.

"Huh?" My eyes swept over the lot. I saw a huge, silvery truck parked at the end of the lot. And then . . . *no cars.*

No cars.

"Where is our car?" My voice came out in a whisper.

We both stared at the empty lot.

"Maybe they went out to bring back breakfast," Artie said.

I frowned. "Maybe." But my heart was pounding. "They would have told us they were going."

"Well . . . they didn't just take off!" Artie said.

I swallowed hard. My mouth suddenly felt dry.

I knocked on the office door and peered through the glass.

"Try the door. Let's just go in," Artie said.

I turned the knob, pushed open the door, and stepped inside with Artie. The room smelled stale and musty. I gazed around quickly. Empty shelves. A bare table. A vending machine with an OUT OF ORDER sign taped to the front.

Then I spotted a man in a blue cap and a red-plaid shirt behind the dark wood counter. He was facing the wall, with his back to us.

I cleared my throat loudly, but he didn't turn around.

"Hello—good morning," I called.

He still didn't move.

"Hey—excuse us," Artie said. And then he punched the bell on the counter. It *dinged* once. Twice.

Again the man didn't move.

I'll bet he's deaf, I thought.

"Sir—?" I moved around to the side of the counter. "Sir?"

He was hunched on a tall wooden stool, shoulders slumped. The blue cap sat high on his head. And his face . . . his face . . .

I stumbled back against the wall and opened my mouth in a shrill scream. *No face! No face at all!*

A yellow skull beneath the cap. Two dark, empty eye sockets. The jaw hanging down in a toothless grin.

"Tammi—what's *wrong?*" Artie shrieked.

I grabbed his hand and lurched to the door. I pulled him outside.

"What's wrong? What *is* it?" Artie demanded.

"We . . . we . . ." The words caught in my throat. "We have to get *out* of here!"

"But—Mom and Dad!" Artie cried. "The man in the office—"

"It wasn't a man!" I shouted. "It was a *skeleton*!"

Artie's eyes narrowed on me. "Huh? That's *crazy*!"

My mind whirred. I took a deep breath and held it. My eyes searched the highway, one direction, then the other. No cars coming.

Where were they? *Where?*

"We have to call the police. They'll help us. They'll come and help us find Mom and Dad, and—"

"We can use the phone in the room," Artie said.

The rain was coming down a little harder, splashing off the red tin roof, pattering over the gravel parking lot.

We burst back into our room. I grabbed the phone off the night table and raised the receiver to my ear. Silence. No dial tone. I pushed 0. Pushed 911. Nothing.

"There's no wire," Artie said. He pulled the phone from my hands. "See? It isn't hooked up to anything."

He tossed the phone onto the bed, and we ran back outside. I searched the parking lot again, praying that our car would be pulling in.

"Where *are* they?" Artie asked shrilly.

I ducked my head into the rain and led the way toward the highway. "We'll find a phone somewhere," I said. "If they don't see us when they get back here, Mom and Dad will wait."

My shoes crunched over the wet gravel. As I walked, a picture flashed into my mind. Last night. Mom with tears suddenly sliding down her cheeks. Mom saying, "You both have to be brave."

What did she mean? Did she know they were going to leave us?

No way. Mom and Dad would never leave us.

Artie and I stopped at the edge of the highway. No cars coming in either direction. Shielding my eyes against the rain with one hand, I squinted to see the other side.

A long, flat green field seemed to stretch forever. And in the distance was a dark building, hazy in the gray light.

A farmhouse?

I placed one hand on Artie's shoulder and pointed with the other. "Maybe they'll have a phone we can use over there."

Artie shivered. His blond hair and the shoulders of his sweatshirt were soaked from the rain. "Let's go," he said.

We jogged across the highway and into the grassy field. The ground was soft and marshy, and our shoes sank into the mud. I kept my eyes on the house in the distance. I saw several smaller buildings beside it.

I heard a rumbling sound behind us on the highway. Our car? I turned back and saw two large red-and-black trucks speed by. I sighed with disappointment and kept walking.

A cemetery appeared as if out of nowhere. Artie and I cried out in surprise. We saw gravestones set in six or seven rows, low in the grass. They were tilted and cracked. Some lay flat on their backs.

"Who would put a graveyard in the middle of a field?" Artie asked.

"Maybe it's where they bury people from that farm," I said, pointing to the house in the distance.

He leaned down to try to read the words on an old stone. As he did, I heard a loud creaking sound, like a rusty door being pulled open.

"Artie!" I gasped as one of the old gravestones toppled over with a *thud*.

"Don't freak," Artie said. "The rain made the ground soft. That's why it fell."

I heard another long *creeeeak*. Another stone toppled over. My breath caught in my throat. I heard a low cracking sound. A large stone tilted forward, then slammed to the ground.

Artie jumped back to my side. "What's happening?"

"I—I don't know," I said.

Then I saw the dirt fly up beside one of the fallen gravestones. And I heard a long, low groan. A groan from *under the ground!*

Frozen to the spot, I saw the dirt crumble and shift in front of another grave. And the tall gravestone toppled onto its back.

"*Ohhhhhhhh.*" Another groan behind me. A weak cry. And then another, a howl of pain from beneath the ground.

"This is crazy!" Artie gasped. "This is *crazy!*"

And then we were running. Running hard, our arms swinging at our sides, our breath wheezing from our open mouths. Running over the wet, muddy field, our shoes slipping, sliding . . . then suddenly I felt myself sinking.

I turned and saw Artie sinking too. His arms thrashed wildly, struggling to pull himself up. But the soft mud was already up to his waist, and he was going down fast.

"It—it's like quicksand!" he wailed.

Down, down. The mud felt so cold, so thick as it rose up over me. I kicked both legs and grabbed frantically at the ground, struggling to escape, struggling to stop sinking.

But it was useless. We were being sucked into a bottomless pit of thick ooze. We're going to *drown* in it! I realized.

"Tammi—do something! I—I can't stay up—" Artie's shrill cry was cut short.

"Hang on! Hang on!" I shrieked. The wet mud rose up to my armpits. My hands grasped furiously at the surface, and my fingers wrapped around a hard object. A tree root?

"Yes!" I squeezed it tightly in my hand. With a groan, I started to pull myself up.

It slipped out of my hand, and I sank back. But I grabbed it again—and pulled myself up . . . up . . . to the surface.

I carefully made my way to Artie. I grabbed his hands and pulled him free of the thick, oozing mud.

And then we were running again. Scrambling like mud crabs, the dark ooze dripping off us.

"Help us! Can anyone help us?" I screamed as we reached the old, brown-shingled farmhouse.

We were answered by a furious snarl from a dog. No. More than one dog, I realized. Sharp, angry growls.

"Dogs—over there!" Artie cried. He pointed to a low wooden shed behind the house.

"Anyone home?" I called, cupping my hands around my mouth. "We—we need help."

I started to the front porch, but Artie pulled me back. "Those dogs," he said, shouting over their angry howls. "Who would lock them up in a tiny shed? They can't breathe in there. They're calling for help."

I pulled him back toward the house. "*We* are the ones who need help! Mom and Dad—" But Artie was already running toward the shed. No arguing with him when it came to dogs. With a sigh, I took off after him.

We reached the shed door at the same time. The dogs howled and raged, barking ferociously. Artie grabbed the door handle. I tugged his arm. "Are you sure you want to do this?"

He nodded. "These dogs are in trouble. I'm not afraid of them. Dogs always like us—remember?"

"Yes, but—"

He pulled open the shed door.

Two enormous black attack dogs—the size of panthers—teeth bared, eyes wild with fury, dove out at us.

I squealed—jumped back and dropped to my knees.

Artie covered his head.

The raging, snarling dogs seemed to hover in midair. Then they dropped heavily to the ground.

"They—they're chained up!" I gasped.

The dogs couldn't run out. The chains around their necks held them back. Now they lowered their heads and glared, still growling angrily.

And a man's voice behind us announced loudly, "I'M SORRY. YOU FLUNK."

"Huh?" Artie and I spun around. We stared at a young man with slicked-back black hair and a deep tan. He wore a charcoal-gray suit, white shirt, and tie. He held an umbrella over his head, even though the rain had slowed to a drizzle.

I squinted at the small badge on his jacket. It read: OFFICIAL JUDGE. "Tammi and Artie, I'm afraid you just failed your test," he said, shaking his head.

"No! Please!" I recognized Mom's voice. And then I saw both of our parents come running from the other side of the house.

"Please!" Mom cried. "Can't you give them another chance?"

"Yes—give them another chance!" Dad demanded.

The dogs growled behind us. The man lowered his umbrella. "Sorry. No second chances. They have failed."

"But—but—" Mom sputtered.

"What is going on here?" I cried.

Dad sighed and shook his head. "All kids have to take car trips," he told me, speaking just above a whisper. "It's a test. The government said all kids must be tested for bravery and intelligence."

"But—why?"

"There's so little space left," Dad said, lowering his eyes. "So little food. So little *everything* to go around. The government decided it had no choice. Only the bravest and smartest kids can survive. Only the bravest and smartest can . . . come home." His voice broke.

Mom wrapped him in a tearful hug.

"You failed because you opened the dog shed," the judge

announced. "You did okay with the graveyard frights and the quicksand. But then you should have gone into the farmhouse. You should have stayed away from the vicious dogs in the shed. Instead, you opened the shed. You showed you were brave—but not smart."

He shook his head. "I'm so sorry. Your parents must return home without you."

Mom burst into loud sobs. Dad was crying too.

"Wait—" Artie cried. "What if we prove we really *are* smart?"

I looked at Artie. Artie looked at me. I knew we were both thinking the exact same thing.

"It's too late," the judge said. "Come with me."

But Artie and I didn't follow him. Instead, we did something really *really* smart.

We grabbed the dog chains—and unleashed the attack dogs.

Growling and snarling, the ferocious dogs tore past us. (Because dogs always like us.) And they dove at the judge. Heaved him to the ground. Ripped at his suit, wrestling, tearing, snapping their jaws, sinking their jagged teeth into his skin.

"Okay! You pass!" He screamed, on his back, kicking and flailing, struggling to protect himself. "You both pass the test! You can go home! Just get them OFF me! Get them off!"

Of course, it was easy to pull the dogs off the poor man. Because dogs always listen to us. We saved his life, and he knew it.

After that, the ride home was a lot of fun. Very relaxed. Lots of jokes and kidding around. And Mom even did her famous folding-the-map routine again, which got howls from all of us.

Sure, there were some rough spots. A few pretty scary moments. But all in all, Artie and I had to agree, this was definitely our family's best car trip ever.

© 2001 Roz Chast

Take Me with You

INTRODUCTION

I don't like going into antique stores, because I know ghosts are lingering there.

I know that the old items on display are haunted by the ghosts of people who owned them. Look around the store. . . .

The silver hairbrush is still held by the hand of the woman who brushed her hair with it so many years ago. The old leather chair isn't empty. There's the man who sat in it day after day, leaning his ghostly head against its soft back.

The antique jeweled beads rattle against the throat of their long-dead owner. And the wooden fire truck is still treasured by the ghostly children who played with it a hundred years ago.

Ghosts everywhere you turn.

I know. I can see them.

This is a story about a father who brings a beat-up old steamer trunk home from an antique store. And guess what is waiting inside. . . .

ILLUSTRATED BY ROZ CHAST

Dad found the old trunk in an antique store and brought it home. The trunk was long and black and covered with dust. The top had a dozen dents and scratches, and the metal clasp was totally rusted.

"Amber, this is a great find!" Dad said.

I groaned. "Bor-ring."

"But this will be perfect for the cruise," he said. "Won't you feel cool boarding the ship with a real old-fashioned steamer trunk?"

"No way," I told him. "It's so old, it will probably make my clothes smell horrible."

But does Dad listen to me? Not too often.

He insisted on dragging the huge trunk to my room. It weighed a ton. I helped him set it down in front of the glass cabinet where I keep my doll collection.

Dust flew everywhere. I sneezed twice, but Dad didn't seem to notice. He was too busy struggling with the clasp.

He gave a mighty tug—and stumbled into the glass cabinet. The dolls all bounced on the shelves, as if they were startled.

"Be careful! My collection!" I shouted.

"I won't hurt your precious dolls," Dad said. He started to the door. "I need a screwdriver."

I reached across the ugly trunk to straighten the dolls. I have eight Barbies in my collection, four Jean dolls, a couple of American Girl dolls, and ten dolls that I bought just because I thought they were cute.

I'm twelve, way too old to play with them now. I only collect them.

But Kat, my eight-year-old sister, is starting her own doll collection. That's why I call her Copy Kat. She always wants what I have.

A few seconds later Dad was back, carrying a screwdriver and a claw hammer. He squatted in front of the old trunk and went to work on the clasp. He hummed to himself as he worked.

"Dad, I'm not taking this ugly trunk on the cruise," I said.

"Let's just see what's inside," he replied. He opened the rusty clasp. Then he made me help him lift up the lid.

"Yuck!" I cried out as a puff of sour, gray air rose up from the trunk like a dust cloud. I know it sounds weird—but the dust made a sighing sound as it escaped the trunk.

Holding my nose, I watched the cloud float up to the ceiling and disappear. "Dad, please!" I begged. "I'm *not* taking that trunk on the cruise! Close it!"

But he was already bending over the trunk, picking around at the bottom. "Wow," he muttered. "Amazing!"

"What's amazing?" I peered into the trunk.

Dad picked up a stack of lace handkerchiefs. They were all yellowed. I saw a pair of old-fashioned black lace-up shoes. Dad lifted out a long gray pleated skirt. Everything looked a hundred years old.

"There's not much in here," Dad said, studying the shoes. "It's as if someone had started to pack and stopped."

"Maybe I could start a smelly-old-clothes collection," I said. It was meant to be a joke. But he thought I was serious.

At dinner he was still talking about the old trunk. "It's a real treasure," he told Mom. "Once I get it cleaned up, Amber will love it."

"What's wrong with a nice *new* suitcase?" I said.

"People always take trunks on cruises," Mom said.

"If Amber has a trunk, I want one too," Kat chimed in.

I sighed. "I can't believe you're making me go on this trip."

I know, I know. I sound like a real whiner. But last summer I went to camp with Amy and Olivia, my two best friends. And I really wanted to go back to that camp again this summer.

I stared at my spaghetti. I hadn't taken a bite. "I'll be the only kid on the ship," I grumbled. "Everyone else will be old geeks."

"Hey! *I'll* be there!" Kat protested.

"You'll find someone to hang out with, Amber," Mom said. "You'll probably make a lot of new friends."

"Why can't we go on a *normal* vacation?" I whined.

"Eat your spaghetti," Dad replied.

After dinner, I hurried upstairs to call Olivia. The musty, sour smell from the trunk greeted me before I stepped into my room.

I stopped at the doorway. The trunk stood open. I raised my eyes to the cabinet—and gasped.

My dolls!

When I left the room, they were standing or sitting in neat rows. Now they were sprawled in every direction. Tumbling off the shelves. Piled on top of each other.

I spotted two Barbies on the floor beside the trunk. Their heads were on backward. Another doll was propped on the top shelf *upside down!*

Pressing my hands against my cheeks, I stared in disbelief. "Kat!" I screamed. "Kat—get up here *right now*!"

Kat came running up the stairs, followed by Mom and Dad. "Amber? What's wrong?" Mom asked.

"Kat messed up all the dolls!" I screamed.

"I did not!" Kat protested.

"Kat was downstairs the whole time," Dad said. "Besides, she would never do something like this."

"I didn't! I didn't!" Kat repeated.

"Well, somebody was up here!" I said. "*Somebody* did this! The cabinet doors are wide open!"

I felt Mom's hands on my shoulders. "Easy," she said quietly.

Scratching his thinning brown hair, Dad turned to me. "I know what happened, Amber. When I bumped into the cabinet earlier, I must have loosened the doors and knocked over a doll."

"But *all* the dolls have been messed up," I said.

Dad frowned. "Well, if one doll falls, it could start a chain reaction, right?"

I stared at the dolls, tossed all over the place. It didn't look like a chain reaction to me.

But how else could it be explained?

≈

It took forever to put the dolls back just the way I like them. Then I talked to Olivia for nearly an hour. When I told her about the dolls, she just laughed and said maybe it was an earthquake.

I tried to get Dad to take the smelly trunk out of my room. But he said he was too busy.

I'm usually a sound sleeper. But that night something woke me up in the middle of the night. A voice. A girl, whispering to me.

"Take . . . me . . . with . . . you."

"Huh?" I jerked straight up, instantly alert. A chill froze the back of my neck. "Who's there?" I asked in a tiny voice.

I reached in the dark for my bed-table lamp and clicked it on. Blinking in the light, I repeated my question. "Who's there?"

No one.

I gazed around the room. The bed-table lamp cast long shadows over the floor. The old trunk was closed. I stared hard at it. The whisper seemed to come from that direction.

I clicked off the light and settled back on my pillow. I started to think maybe I'd been dreaming—when I felt a blast of cold air and heard the whisper again.

"Take . . . me . . . with . . . you—please."

The trunk! The voice had to be coming from the trunk!

"Who's there?" I shouted. "Where are you?"

The bedroom door swung open, and Mom and Dad came bursting into the room. "Amber—what's wrong?"

I sat up in bed, gripping the sheet between my hands. "A girl whispered," I told them. "She whispered, *'Take me with you.'*"

I could see right away that they didn't believe me.

"I heard whispers too!" Kat called from down the hall.

"Kat—go back to sleep," Dad shouted.

Mom stepped up to me and smoothed my hair back tenderly. "You were dreaming," she said. "You're nervous about the cruise. So you dreamed about it."

"I'm not nervous about the stupid cruise!" I screamed. "Open the trunk. Her voice sounded as if it came from the trunk."

Dad lifted the trunk lid. "Oh, yeah. There's a whole bunch of kids in here," he said. "Having a party."

"It isn't funny!" I shouted angrily.

"Go back to sleep," Mom said. "Everything is okay."

I let them go back to their room. I wasn't going to argue. I knew they wouldn't believe me no matter what.

I tried to fall back asleep but I was totally alert, listening . . . listening for the girl's whisper. Finally I buried my face in the pillow and forced myself to sleep.

≈

Thursday morning I woke up before my alarm went off. I felt as if I hadn't slept a minute. Yawning, I made my way into the bathroom. I clicked on the light—and gasped.

I blinked at the words on the medicine-cabinet mirror. Words scrawled across the glass in red lipstick.

Take me with you.

"Mom! Dad!" I shouted for them.

They were already having their breakfast. I heard the chairs scrape in the kitchen. They came running up the stairs.

"Look!" I pointed frantically at the scrawled words on the mirror. "That's what the girl was whispering! The same words!"

They poked their heads into the bathroom. I saw Dad's eyes go to the lipstick tube on the side of the sink. My lipstick tube.

Mom shook her head. "Amber, that doesn't prove anything," she said softly. "Writing words on the mirror with your lipstick isn't going to convince Dad and me that the voice you heard last night was real. It was a nightmare. Everyone has nightmares."

"But I didn't write those words!" I said.

"We know you're tense about the cruise," Dad said, patting me on the head as if I were five—not twelve. "But you have to stop this."

"We have to run," Mom said. "We have to buy swimsuits for the ship. Amber, clean off the mirror and go to school."

They hurried away. I listened to the door slam behind them.

My parents didn't believe me. But I knew the truth.

I ran into my room. I pulled on my clothes in two seconds flat.

My heart pounded like crazy. The voice last night seemed to come from the old trunk. Was the trunk haunted or something? No way I wanted to be alone and find out!

I was nearly out the back door when I felt a burst of cold air on the back of my neck.

And then I heard the whispers again.

A girl's voice. Right behind me. Right in my ear.

"Take . . . me . . . with . . . you.

"Take . . . me . . . with . . . you."

≈

I brought Amy and Olivia home with me after school. I really didn't want to be alone.

They made me show them the old trunk. When I pulled up the lid, I expected a hideous ghost to leap out at me.

But except for the old clothes we'd found, the trunk was empty. My friends agreed with me that it smelled disgusting.

"If you cleaned it up, this would make a good camp trunk," Olivia said.

"But I'm not going to camp!" I wailed.

They both hugged me. I knew they really felt sorry for me.

"Hope you don't get seasick and spend the whole time barfing," Amy said.

Wow. That cheered me up a lot.

≈

That night at dinner I begged Dad to take the trunk back to the store. He said he'd try to get around to it, maybe Friday or Saturday.

My parents went out to visit friends. When I went to bed, I left my desk lamp on. I thought it might keep the whisperer away.

But I was wrong.

I had just settled into bed when I felt a gust of cold wind chill the room. *"Take me with you . . . please. . . ."*

I opened my mouth to scream, but no sound came out.

The air grew colder. A strange stillness fell over the room. And in the hush I heard the whispered words one more time.

"Take . . . me . . . with . . . you."

Then a cloudy figure floated out of the open trunk. A girl. An old-fashioned-looking girl with long, dark ringlets framing her face.

Dressed in black. Her eyes big and dark and deep.

"No! No—please! Go away! Wh-what do you want?" I gazed up at her in horror as she floated above me.

The light formed a ring around her dark, pretty face. The eyes gazed down at me . . . such sad, empty eyes.

"Thank you," she whispered. *"Thank you for letting me out of my trunk. I've been locked in there so long."*

"You're a ghost? You're really a ghost?" I gasped. "Go away! Please—don't hurt me!"

She floated closer. *"Take me with you,"* she repeated. Her eyes grew even wider. They appeared to sink deep into her head. Her dark hair floated around her face as if she were swimming underwater.

"Go away!" I said again. "Please—go away!"

"Take me. You must take me with you."

"NO!" I cried. "I can't! Go away!"

I raised both hands to bat her away. My hand grazed her arm. She felt so cold. Her skin was freezing cold!

"Please—don't hurt me!" I pleaded again. "Don't hurt me!"

Her eyes glowed. *"I hope I don't have to,"* she said.

I tried to jump out of bed. To run. But she floated close. And the cold air around her . . . it held me in place.

"I never got to go on my journey," she whispered. *"So long ago . . . I was going to visit my grandparents in Scotland. I started to pack the trunk. But then I fell ill. And I died. Poor me. I died before the ship sailed."*

"I—I'm sorry," I replied, still shivering. "But, please—I can't help you. Please—"

"Take me with you. You MUST take me! Take me in the trunk! I can't stay out of the trunk for long—or I will disappear forever. Take me! Take me with you!"

"No!" I opened my mouth and tried to scream. But a heavy blast of sour air muffled my shout. The ghostly girl floated low over my bed.

"I won't take you! I won't!" I insisted, my voice trembling.

Her expression turned angry. Her pale lips curled in a sneer. *"You WILL take me,"* she rasped. *"Because I'll be YOU!"*

"What do you mean?" I gasped.

But already I felt her pressing down on me. Felt a cold, heavy sensation that began at the top of my head. A frozen weight sliding into my brain.

I couldn't keep my eyes open. Suddenly it took an effort to breathe. I felt the cold weight of her, pressing into my brain, my body.

"I'm possessing you, Amber," she whispered. *"I'm taking over now. And I will go on the cruise in your place."*

"No . . . "

The room filled with clouds. Heavy gray clouds. I couldn't see the light from the desk.

"I'm going on the cruise, Amber," the girl said. *"In a few seconds you won't feel anything. You won't feel anything at all. You'll be gone."*

Nooooooo.

I thought I screamed the word, but I heard it only in my mind.

I have to fight her off. I have to push her away.

Gathering all my strength, I heaved myself up from the bed—and staggered to my feet.

I'm still in control, I realized. I'm still in control of my own body.

"Don't fight me, Amber," the ghost warned. *"You can't win."*

Yes, I can, I decided. Yes . . . yes . . .

Battling her, battling the weight that pushed down on me, I lurched blindly across the bedroom.

I reached out both arms, and through the cold, deep blackness I grabbed on to something. I grabbed a doll in each hand. Grabbed them off the top of the cabinet and clutched them to my chest.

"These are mine!" I cried, finding my voice. "These are mine—and they prove I'm still me!"

To my surprise the darkness lifted, like clouds floating out of the sky, and I saw the ghost girl beside me. Back in her old clothes. Back in her ghostly body. A startled, angry look on her face.

Angry because I had pushed her out.

I saw her stagger back a step. Saw the flash of fear in her eyes. And I dove forward. Forced my body—*my* body!—to leap. I slammed into her with all my strength.

She opened her mouth in a gasp as she fell back into the trunk with a startled groan.

Her dark hair flew over her face. Her body appeared to fold up. I heaved the trunk lid shut and snapped the latch.

Then I threw myself on top of the trunk. Wheezing, panting, my heart racing, my entire body dripping with sweat.

I held on to the trunk as if it were a life raft. And waited. Waited to see if the ghost girl would rise up howling from the trunk.

Waited . . . struggling to breathe . . . forcing my heartbeats to slow.

No. She couldn't escape. I had locked her in. I had defeated her. I had sent her back to the darkness of the trunk forever.

Wearily I climbed to my feet and staggered to my bed.

"Amber? What's all the noise up there?"

Mom and Dad had returned. I let out a long sigh. "Nothing, Dad," I called down. "Everything is okay now."

≈

Sunday morning the sunlight poured into my room. I peered out at a solid blue sky. Birds sang in the trees.

"Beautiful morning to start a cruise," Mom said.

She and I left for the pier after breakfast. Dad and Kat stayed behind to deal with the luggage.

As Mom and I boarded the enormous, white ship, I suddenly felt excited. I don't believe it, I thought. This ship is so cool. And there are other kids my age. This is going to be awesome!

Kat and I were going to share a cabin. It was next door to Mom and Dad's. When the white-uniformed steward showed me inside, I gasped.

It was totally beautiful. Luxurious leather furniture. A TV and VCR. And our own private deck where Kat and I could sit and watch the ocean go by.

Wow!

A short while later I was checking out the candy bars in the mini bar. I heard a knock on my cabin door. It swung open, and Dad and Kat walked in.

Dad beamed at me. "Like the cabin, Amber?"

"I love it!" I cried. "It's truly amazing, Dad! I think I was wrong about this cruise."

That made his smile grow even wider.

"Surprise!" Kat cried. "Guess what I brought."

Dad motioned to a steward outside the door.

"You didn't want it," Kat said, "so I got it! I got the great old trunk!"

My mouth dropped open. "What?"

The porter slid the trunk into the center of the cabin.

Dad bent down in front of it. He grabbed the latch and popped it up.

"Here, Kat," he said. "Let me open it for you."

My Imaginary Friend

INTRODUCTION

Go away, Max. I don't have time to talk now.

No, really. Max, give me a break. Go away and let me write. I'll talk to you when I'm finished, okay?

Max—please!

Sorry, readers. Max is my imaginary friend, and he's driving me crazy today.

Do you think I'm too old to have an imaginary friend? Yes. So do I. But someone should tell that to Max!

Max—get away from my keyboard. I'm going to write a story about a boy who has an imaginary friend—a *very dangerous* imaginary friend.

No. You can't help me. Go away. I mean it, Max.

Get away from the computer! Go away. *GO AWAY!*

ILLUSTRATED BY CLAY PATRICK MCBRIDE

David turned away from his computer and stared across the bedroom at Shawn. "Why are you lying there like a dead fish?" he asked. "Come over here. We'll play a game."

Shawn groaned and pulled the blankets up to his chin. "I don't feel well."

"Boo-hoo," David said. "Get over here, Shawn, or else—"

The bedroom door swung open and David's mom stepped in. She was short and a little chubby, like David, with tight ringlets of black hair that bobbed on her head when she walked.

"Hey, Mom. How's it going?" David asked.

She didn't answer. She leaned down and spread her palm over Shawn's narrow forehead. Shawn didn't look anything like David. He was very thin, with a mop of straight blond hair that always hung in his eyes. "Your head is cool," she said softly. "I don't think you have a fever."

"Feel Travis's head," Shawn said. "He's sick too."

Mom groaned and rolled her eyes. But she reached across the bed and spread her hand out again. "No temperature. He's fine," she said.

"Shawn isn't that sick," David said. "He's probably faking. You know. He always wants attention."

His mom straightened the blankets. She turned to the window. "Why on earth did you open that?" she asked. "It's freezing cold in here."

"Travis said he was hot," Shawn replied. "Travis made me do it."

Mom frowned at Shawn. "I'm a little worried about you," she said, pressing her hands to her waist. "You're twelve years old, Shawn. It's really time you got rid of your imaginary friend."

She crossed the room and shut the window. She straightened some books on David's bookcase. Then she fluffed Shawn's pillow.

"Hey, Mom, what's for dinner?" David asked.

But she was out the bedroom door, closing it behind her.

"Why did she say that about me?" Travis demanded as soon as the door was shut. "Why did she say I have to go?"

"Don't worry," Shawn replied. "I won't get rid of you."

David stood up and crossed to the foot of Shawn's bed. "You *should* get rid of Travis. You're worrying Mom with all that invisible-friend stuff," he said.

"Why don't you mind your own business?" Shawn snapped. "You're not the boss. You can't tell me what to do."

Travis let out a long, loud yawn. "Bor-ring!" he said. "It's totally boring lying around doing nothing. Let's sneak out."

Shawn sat up in bed. He brushed his hair away from his eyes. "Sneak out? But it's late. We could get in major trouble."

Travis grinned at him. "Only if we're caught."

David watched Shawn pull on jeans and a sweatshirt. "Don't listen to Travis. He always gets you into a mess. You're making a big mistake," he said.

"Your *face* is a big mistake," Shawn replied. He pulled open the window, threw his leg over the sill, and climbed out into the night.

David didn't want to go out, but he pulled on his coat and followed Shawn. Maybe I can help keep him out of trouble, he thought.

They stepped into a cold, moonless night. The wind swirled around the houses and howled through the trees. Somewhere down the block a dog barked. Dead leaves scuttled around their legs and crackled beneath their shoes.

"I don't like being out this late," David said, shivering. "I think we should go back."

"Travis doesn't want to go back," Shawn replied. "Travis is bored."

They stopped in front of the Harpers' house on the next block.

The driveway light sent a rectangle of yellow over the side of the garage.

They saw a tall ladder and a stack of paint cans. Half the garage wall had been painted yellow.

"Let's help paint the garage," Travis said.

"No way!" Shawn protested. "If Mr. Harper catches us . . ."

"Why are you always so scared?" Travis sneered. "Poor little *Shawny Baby* is frightened? Don't you ever want to have any fun?"

Shawn turned and started up the driveway. "Okay. Let's paint," he said.

David ran after Shawn. "No— please!" he begged. "Please stop!"

But Shawn pried open the paint cans. He picked up a brush and dipped it into the can of black paint. Then he painted a big smiley face on the garage wall.

He and Travis played tic-tac-toe on the wall in green paint. Then Shawn wrote Travis's name in big red letters. They giggled and danced as they painted.

But they stopped giggling when a car pulled up the driveway and the twin beams of the headlights rolled over them.

Shawn and Travis froze for just a second. Then they tossed the paintbrushes to the ground and took off—vanishing through the hedge at the side of the yard.

David's dad jumped out of the car and stormed toward the garage. Even in the dark David could see the angry look on his face.

"It's not my fault!" David cried. "Really, Dad. Shawn did all the painting. I—I just followed him. I begged him to stop."

Dad glared furiously at David. His dark mustache flared up and down as he gritted his teeth. "This has got to stop, David. Your mother will be so disappointed in you."

"But it wasn't my idea!" David protested. "You've got to believe me. It was Shawn. Why don't you ever blame *him*?"

≈

After school the next day David followed Shawn out of the building. Low clouds hung overhead, threatening snow. The ground was hard and frosty.

David pulled his parka hood down over his head. "I have to go straight home," David grumbled. "I've been grounded—because of last night."

"Travis wants to go home a different way today," Shawn said. "Just for fun."

David squinted at him suspiciously. "Which different way?" he asked.

"He wants to go over the old railroad trestle," Shawn said, stepping ahead.

"No way!" David cried.

"It *is* kind of dangerous," Shawn agreed. "The wood planks are all rotting. That trestle could collapse at any time."

Travis glared at Shawn and shook his head. "Why are you always the biggest chicken on earth? Don't you ever get tired of being such a wimp?"

"I'm not a wimp. I'll show you," Shawn replied.

Fat snowflakes started to fall as they stepped up to the old wooden trestle. It had once been a railroad bridge over a wide creek. But the creek had dried up. And no trains had come through town in many years.

Many of the boards were cracked and broken. Others had fallen away, leaving huge gaping holes. The whole trestle trembled in the wind.

David's hood had fallen back. He brushed snow from his bushy black hair. "You can't do this," he told Shawn. "No one is allowed on this bridge. It's too dangerous."

"But Travis says—" Shawn started.

"Travis is *imaginary*!" David screamed. "Please—just this once—don't listen to him!"

He grabbed Shawn by the shoulder. "Shape up!" he cried. "You can't keep listening to Travis. He's going to kill you! He's going to kill us both!"

Shawn shook himself free and ran to follow Travis onto the wooden trestle. As he started to make his way across, the planks creaked and squeaked. A piece of the wooden railing broke off in Shawn's hand.

The bridge trembled in a strong gust of wind. The fat snowflakes had already left a powdery cover on the wooden planks.

I can't watch, David told himself. His whole body was trembling. He shut his eyes. And then opened them with a gasp when he heard a long, cracking sound.

Shawn was nearly to the other side. But David could see the trestle shaking hard, see the planks giving way on both sides.

It's collapsing! he realized.

Waving his arms, David leaped onto the trestle. "Hurry!" he shouted. "Shawn—hurry! Move!" David chased after him, shouting at the top of his lungs.

Crack crack crack crack.

The planks were popping off, dropping to the snowy ground below.

Shawn dove to the other side. He slid on the slippery grass. Safe.

David stumbled on the trembling wooden trestle. His foot caught in a hole where a plank had fallen away.

Crack crack craaaaack.

More planks fell away. David gripped the railing. He struggled to stay on his feet as the old bridge swayed wildly from side to side.

Two more planks dropped out—nearly under his feet. He jumped back, gripping the shaking rail.

"I'm trapped!" he called. "Help! Get help! I'm trapped here—and it's going down!"

He squinted through the falling snow to the far side of the trestle. "Shawn? Where are you? Shawn? I need help!"

A few seconds later David heard the sirens. Three red fire trucks squealed to a stop at one end of the trestle. Yellow-uniformed firefighters, their faces grim, jumped down from the trucks. Some of them began to make a rope harness to pull David to safety.

Gripping the rail, David listened in panic to the trestle creaking and cracking. Hurry! Please—hurry! he thought, watching the firefighters work.

Then he saw his dad jogging over the snow. His face was red. Puffs of steam floated from his mouth as he ran. "David!" he shouted over the voices of the firefighters. "I don't believe this!"

"Dad—it's not what you think!" David shouted back. "It wasn't my idea at all. I was trying to rescue Shawn. You've got to believe me this time. You've *got* to!"

≈

David paced angrily back and forth in his room. He kicked the wall. He pounded his fist against his closet door. "I may spend the rest of my life in this room," he complained to Shawn. "I'm grounded forever—and it's all your fault."

Shawn didn't reply.

David bumped up to him and shoved his face into Shawn's. "Travis is the troublemaker. This is all his fault. He has to go, Shawn. Do you hear me? He's dangerous. He's really dangerous. Your imaginary friend has to go—now!"

Shawn sighed and shrugged his shoulders. "Yeah, I guess," he said. "You're probably right. But what can I do?"

Shawn turned to Travis, who was sitting on the windowsill, staring out the open window at the moon. "Let's get out of here," Travis said.

≈

A few minutes later they were out in the frosty night, their breath misting in front of them. They gazed at the fishing pond behind the park where Travis had led them.

A thin layer of ice gleamed under the yellow moonlight. A thousand little cracks stretched over the silvery surface. Water splashed where the delicate ice had broken apart.

"What are we doing here?" David asked, zipping his parka as high as it would go. "This is crazy!"

Then he caught the frightened look on Shawn's face.

What was happening? Shawn was backing up, backing toward the pond.

"Travis—stop it!" Shawn cried. He turned to David. "Stop him, David. Travis—he's forcing me onto the ice!"

"Stop!" David cried, panic choking his throat. "The ice is too thin. It can't hold anyone."

"Why are you doing this?" Shawn cried. He staggered back. One foot landed on the crackling surface.

"I'm taking over," Travis said. "I'm tired of being the imaginary one. From now on *I'm* going to be the real one, Shawn. And *you* will be my invisible friend!"

"Noooo!" Shawn wailed. "You can't do that! I'm real! You're just imaginary!"

"Not anymore," Travis sneered. "I'm taking over now. It's time for you to go. Good-bye, Shawn."

He grabbed Shawn by the shoulders. Grunting, crying out, the two of them wrestled onto the surface of the ice.

David opened his mouth in a shrill scream as the ice cracked. Like a broken mirror it split into dozens of jagged shards.

Still wrestling, Shawn and Travis plunged into the dark water.

"No—no—no!" David chanted, shivering in terror. "No—no—please!"

And then he forced himself to move. He dove onto the ice. Threw himself into the open hole, into the frozen water.

His heart thudding in his chest, he searched under the surface for Shawn.

David's body started to turn numb in the icy water. He couldn't feel his arms . . . his legs . . . he couldn't breathe. . . .

He forced himself to keep searching. But the darkness surrounded him. He couldn't see a thing in the inky blackness.

He thrashed out, searching for Shawn with his hands. Reaching out frantically. Groping for Shawn in the icy darkness.

He stayed down until his chest felt ready to explode. Then he burst back to the surface, choking, gasping for air.

"Where are you? Shawn? Where did you go? Help—somebody! Oh, help!"

≈

"David is very lucky that a neighbor heard his shouts," Dr. Kline said. "He was very lucky to be pulled out. Another few seconds and he would have drowned."

David's dad shook his head sadly. He turned to David in the hospital bed. "How did this happen?" he asked. "How did you fall into the pond?"

"I—I tried to save them," David replied. "Shawn and Travis. Are they okay, Dad? I tried to save them, but I couldn't see them. It was too dark . . . too dark."

"Try to rest, David," Dr. Kline said. He walked David's dad out into the hall. "Who are Shawn and Travis?" the doctor asked.

David's dad tugged at his mustache. He let out a long, weary sigh. "Shawn and Travis are David's imaginary friends," he explained.

Dr. Kline's eyes went wide. "Really?"

"Yes. Ever since David's mom and I divorced, ever since she moved away, David imagines that she's still there. He still talks to her. And he spends all his time talking to these two imaginary boys."

David's dad took a deep breath. "I've tried to get help, Dr. Kline. I just don't know what to do."

The two men stood staring at each other. From back in the room they could hear David's voice. . . .

"Shawn. Travis. Look at all the trouble you got me in. You went too far this time. You landed me in the hospital!"

"Bor-ring!" David heard Travis reply. "Let's bust out of this place. Come on, David. No one is looking. *Run!*"

Losers

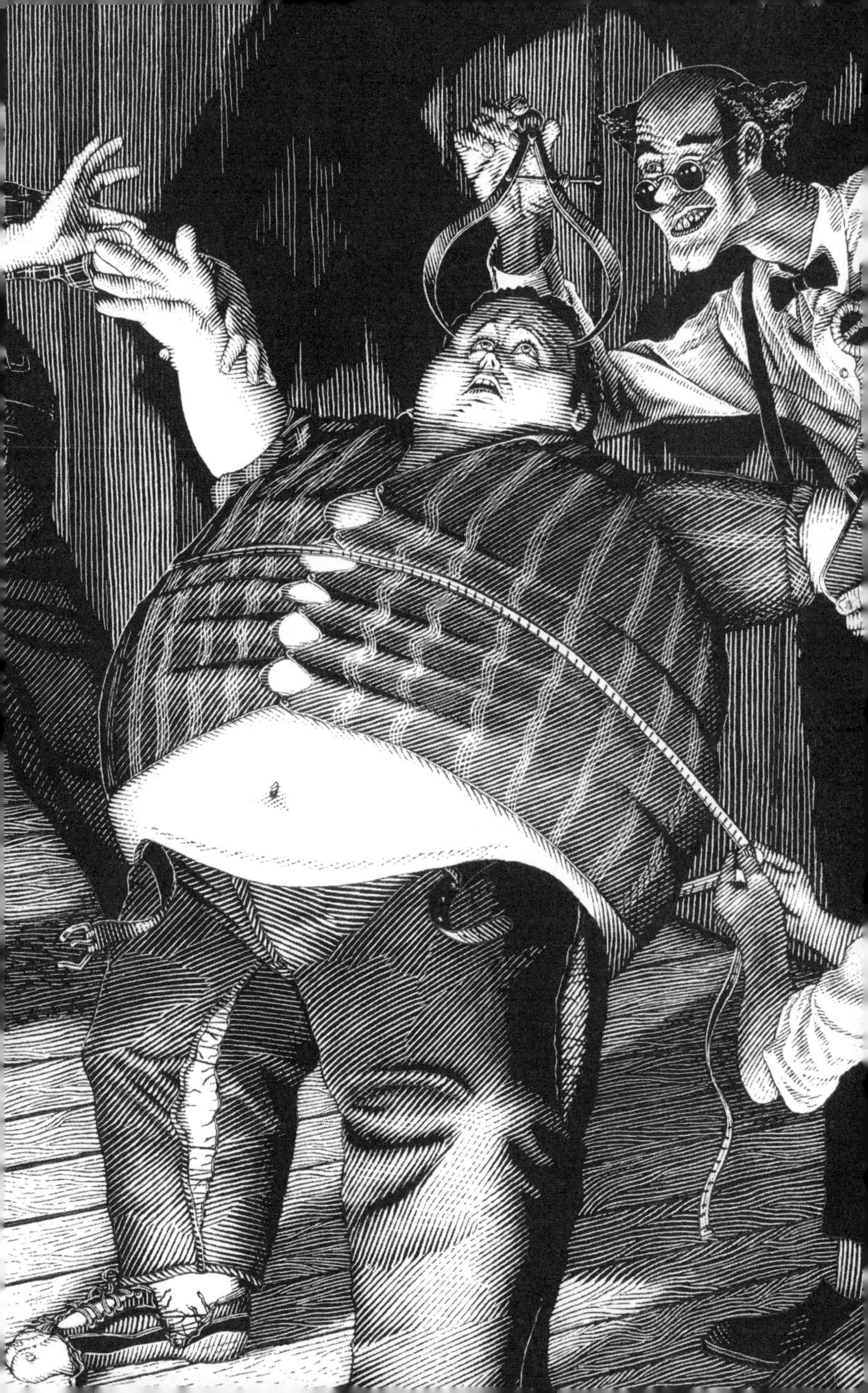

INTRODUCTION

Where do story ideas come from? This one came from a memory that has always haunted me.

I grew up in Columbus, Ohio. Every summer my friends and I looked forward to the Ohio State Fair. We loved everything about it—the great junk food, the giant pumpkins and squashes and melons, the demolition derbies, the carnival rides, the award-winning horses, cows, and fat, sloppy hogs.

One night we stayed very late. Somehow I got separated from everyone. The fair was closing. The lights were dimming. I ran along a back fence, searching for my friends.

Suddenly a huge man in a baggy black suit stepped into my path. His face was big and round and wrinkled, like a prize cabbage. "Hurry," he called to me. "This way! Hurry! You're just in time!"

I stopped and stared at him. The fairgrounds were nearly empty. *What did he want?*

"Hurry—you're just in time," he whispered. "This way!"

A chill ran down my back. I turned and ran. I heard the man laughing behind me—cold, cruel laughter.

Some nights I still hear that laughter. I thought of that cabbage-faced man in the dark fairgrounds when I wrote this story.

ILLUSTRATED BY PATRICK ARRASMITH

My friend Pete and I go to the Washoo County Fair every fall just to laugh. Believe me, it's a hoot. You should see the weird things they have at this fair. And the people are even weirder!

Pete's cousin Franny always comes with us too. But Franny *likes* the fair! She says Pete and I are stuck-up snobs. "You shouldn't judge people," Franny says. That just makes us laugh even more.

We're twelve now. But the three of us have been going to the fair since we were in kindergarten. Believe me, it just doesn't get any stranger than this.

"Colin, check this out!" Pete poked me in the ribs. We had just entered the dairy barn. We like to make faces at the cows. "Over here," Pete said, pointing.

I stared at the shiny yellow statue in front of us. "Oh, wow. George Washington carved out of butter."

"Are you sure that's George Washington?" Pete asked. "It kinda looks like your mom!"

"No!" I cried. "It looks a *lot* like my mom!"

The two of us fell on the floor laughing.

"I don't think it's funny," Franny said. "Someone worked really hard on this."

"Why work so hard on something that's just going to melt?" I said. "How dumb is that?"

We made our way down the long row of pens, mooing at the cows and making faces at them. The cows didn't seem to mind. But some of their owners gave us dirty looks.

"You two are embarrassing me," Franny said. She led the way back outside.

It was a cool, breezy evening. A bright half-moon hung low in the starry sky.

"Check out that goof over there," Pete said. "He's eating four corn dogs at once! Two in each hand!"

"How about that geek?" I said, pointing. "He's wearing black socks with sandals. Nice look, dude!"

"Stop it!" Franny scolded. "You can't judge people by their looks or how they dress."

"Of course you can!" Pete said.

We wandered into the next building and saw rows of tables holding giant cabbages. Some of these cabbages were as big as cars!

Across from us a light flashed. A woman was snapping photo after photo of a fat green-and-yellow cabbage.

"Wish I'd brought *my* camera!" I exclaimed.

"The woman looks just like her cabbage," Pete said. "All green and wrinkled!"

"Why don't you kids move on?" a big red-faced man said. He had both hands on his cabbage, like he was petting it.

Suddenly it grew very quiet in the building. The people behind the tables stood up, as if at attention.

I turned and saw two men and a woman approaching. They wore blue blazers and had bright-red badges pinned to their fronts that read: COUNTY JUDGE.

"Cool! We're in time for the judging," Franny said.

"Bor-ring," Pete groaned. "Let's get out of here."

"No. Wait," I said. I bent down and picked up a fat purple worm I'd seen crawling on the dirt floor. When the farmer turned away, I slipped the worm onto a front leaf of his cabbage.

"Okay. We can go now," I said. As soon as we were outside, I burst into a giggling fit. "I don't think that guy is going to win any ribbons today."

"Look! Hogs!" Pete cried, pointing to the next barn. "Hogs are great. Let's go check 'em out."

We pushed our way through a group of little kids with ice slurpies pressed to their faces. Then we stepped into the hog barn. What a racket. The hogs were squealing and honking.

Pete and I got down on our hands and knees and squealed and honked right back at them.

"Why don't you guys grow up?" Franny said.

No way. It was a riot! One stupid hog tried to charge us. Grunting and squawking, he rammed his head right into the wall of his pen. That got the next hog worked up too. He came charging forward.

"Stampede!" I shouted. "Run for your lives! Hog stampede!"

We were laughing so hard, Pete and I nearly fell into the pen.

I saw some hog owners running across the barn after us. They looked pretty upset. So we took off. Outside, we tossed our heads back and roared out shrill honks and squeals.

"Not funny," Franny moaned, rolling her eyes. "Remind me not to come with you two next year."

"Remind yourself to get a sense of humor!" Pete told her.

She tried to slug him, but he danced away.

We made our way into a long tent at the edge of the fairgrounds and saw row after row of gigantic orange and yellow squashes.

"Man, these are ugly!" I said, walking down the long aisle. "They're all lumpy and gross."

I squeezed the end of a big orange-and-green-striped squash. "Yuck. This one is kind of soft." I turned to Pete with a grin. "Do you still have that marking pen?"

He pulled the black marking pen from his jeans pocket.

I took it from him. I made sure no one was watching. Then I wrote **LOSER** in big black letters on the side of the squash.

"That's *awful!*" Franny cried. "I can't take this anymore. You both are horrible!" She hurried away, shaking her head angrily.

I picked up a big squash. "Hey, come back! This one looks just like you!" I called.

Pete and I had a major giggling fit. "She'll get over it," Pete said.

To my surprise, a chubby man in a floppy straw hat stepped in front of us. He wore an ugly red-plaid shirt that hung over baggy, wrinkled white shorts. "This way," he said. "Hurry."

"Huh? What do you want?" I asked.

"I've been watching you. Come this way," he said.

Pete and I tried to step around him. But he blocked us with his big stomach.

He pulled off the straw hat, revealing a nest of bright-red hair. His round face was covered with freckles.

He motioned with the hat. "Hurry. Here's the Youth Building."

He led us to the back of a long, low white building. Then he used the hat to herd us through a narrow door.

Pete and I stepped into a small, dimly lit room. "Hey—where are we?" I cried. "What's up with this?"

"I think you boys are winners," the man drawled, scratching his head. A big grin crossed his pudgy face. "Yep. I got me two winners." He pushed the straw hat back on his head and let out a whoop.

My throat suddenly felt dry. I had a bad feeling about this. "Pete and I have to go now," I said. I started to the door.

Again the man blocked our path. "Just sit tight," he said. "Everything will be fine. You'll see. My name is MacColley, by the way. You can call me Mac. I'll be right back."

He bounced out the door and slammed it shut behind him.

I darted to the door and tried the handle. It didn't budge. "We—we're locked in," I told Pete.

"This is crazy," Pete muttered. "What does that guy want?"

I gazed around. The room was small and narrow. A bare concrete floor. No furniture at all. I saw shelves at the far end. They seemed to be filled with large glass jars.

"Hey—do you hear that?" Pete whispered.

Yes. I heard cheers and laughter. They seemed to be coming from another part of the building.

I listened hard. I heard music. Then loud applause.

"It sounds like some kind of show," Pete said.

I shrugged and crossed the room to the shelves. "Check out these big jars," I said. "Looks like some kind of pickled stuff."

And then I let out a horrified gasp.

"It . . . it can't be," I said.

But yes. Floating in the jar in front of me was a hand. A smooth white hand. Pale and small.

A human hand.

"Pete—"

"I—I see it," Pete stammered.

My eyes moved over the shelves of jars. Each one contained a human hand, floating in some kind of thick jelly.

"Oh, wow." My legs suddenly felt weak and shaky. "Do you think they're real?"

"They . . . look real," Pete said.

Light poured into the room as the door opened. The man in the straw hat stepped in. He held two paper cones filled with blue candy in his hands. It looked like blue cotton candy.

"Brought you boys a snack." He shoved the cones into our hands.

"Are those real?" I asked, pointing to the jars.

He shook his head. "Don't sweat those, boys. They're just for display."

"We have to go," I said. "Really. We're late, and—"

Beneath the brim of his straw hat, MacColley narrowed his eyes at us. "Don't be in such a hurry, boys. Have your snack first."

I looked at the blue, sticky stuff. "If we eat the cotton candy, can we go?"

"Why, sure," MacColley drawled. "Go ahead. Enjoy."

I heard more laughter and applause through the wall. MacColley stared at us, his arms crossed over his big stomach, waiting for us to eat the cotton candy.

We raised the cones to our faces and bit off blue chunks.

"Sweet, huh?" the man asked.

I nodded and bit off another chunk. It was very sweet. Tasted great. But it wasn't cotton candy. It didn't melt away in your mouth the way cotton candy does. It was very chewy. And it seemed to fluff up as you chewed it.

"Eat the whole thing, boys," MacColley urged.

The candy swelled up in my mouth until it was a huge ball. I struggled to choke it down. It was kind of like trying to eat an inflated balloon. The more I chewed, the bigger it got.

Pete gagged and tried to spit out a hunk. But it stuck to his teeth and the roof of his mouth. It was too big to spit out!

Finally I choked the last of mine down. I felt stuffed! "Can we go now?" I asked.

Grinning, MacColley nodded. "Sure thing. It's just about time."

"Time for what?" Pete asked.

MacColley opened a door on the far wall and motioned us through it. We walked down a long, dark tunnel. As we walked, the cheers and laughter grew louder.

Where is he taking us? I wondered. *This isn't the way outside.*

I wanted to run, but suddenly my legs felt like lead weights.

At the end of the tunnel MacColley pushed open a door. We

stared into bright light. "Here you go, boys," he said. He pushed us into the light.

"Whoa!" I cried out when I saw the bleachers full of people. It was a big arena.

A loud cheer went up as MacColley pushed Pete and me to the platform. I heard laughter and some boos.

"What's going on?" I demanded.

"Up you go," MacColley ordered. "You're just in time for the judging. Good luck. Make me proud."

"Excuse me? Judging?" A wave of dread swept over me.

"Colin, let's get out of here," Pete whispered.

Too late. We were already standing on the stage next to two other kids. One was the tallest, skinniest boy I had ever seen. He looked our age, but he was at least ten feet tall.

A girl, about fifteen, stood next to the skinny guy. She wore blue jeans and a pink T-shirt and had shoulder-length brown hair—sprouting from her face! It grew out of her cheeks, her chin, her ears. It even grew out of her nostrils. Man, was she gross.

Four spotlights sent beams of blinding white light over us.

Applause and shouts roared up from the audience as the tall boy and hairy girl walked off the stage.

I shielded my eyes from the bright light and tried to see who was out there.

I saw farmers in bib overalls and bright-plaid work shirts. I recognized a couple of the hog owners who had chased us away. And the man whose cabbage I'd dropped the worm on.

Two women held prize squashes in their laps. The big men beside them had blueberry stains around their mouths and chins.

All the people Pete and I had made fun of. They all seemed to be in the audience, staring down at us, grinning and clapping.

"Pete—let's get out of here!" I cried.

"I . . . I can't move," Pete said.

"Huh? What's your problem?" I asked. And then I let out a cry as I saw my hands. My fingers had ballooned to the size of hot dogs! My hands were totally swollen.

I raised them close to study them—and realized that my arms were huge too. I felt my stomach swell. It bulged right out of my T-shirt and kept growing.

"Pete—" I gasped. Pete was *enormous!* He looked like a balloon in the Thanksgiving Day parade.

"Look at those big boys!" a man in the crowd shouted. "Those are growing boys!"

Everyone laughed.

"Help! Let us mmmmph mmmmph!" I tried to shout. But my tongue swelled up till it filled my mouth.

I raised my big hands to my head. My head was huge too. My round stomach bounced in front of me.

I look like a cabbage, I realized.

I can't talk. I can't move. I'm . . . I'm just like a cabbage!

"Ha ha! You can roll that boy home!" someone shouted. The arena exploded with laughter.

I turned my heavy blob of a head to Pete. He bounced on his feet like a huge beach ball.

Then I heard footsteps behind me. The crowd grew silent as four men in overalls climbed onto the stage.

The grim-faced judges surrounded Pete and me. One of them grabbed my hand and squeezed it. Another judge wrapped a tape measure around one of my fat legs. "Forty-two," he called out.

I tried to step away from them, but I was too heavy to move.

A judge slipped one of those prongy metal calipers over my head and measured my head. "Eighty-four," he shouted.

Several people in the crowd booed.

"Reject!" a woman called out.

A judge pushed back my sausagelike fingers until they cracked. Another judge tapped my flabby knees with a hammer.

"MMMMMMPH!" I wanted to cry out in pain. But my fat tongue filled my mouth. I couldn't make a sound.

The judges jabbed my back and poked my stomach. One of them squeezed my nose until tears poured from my eyes.

"Losers!" a man shouted from high in the bleachers. "Throw out the losers!"

"Give them a chance!" I heard MacColley shout. "These are my boys! Give them a chance!"

"Hold still," a judge ordered. "I need to take a skin sample."

Oh no, I thought. A skin sample? What is he going to do?

I struggled to move—in any direction. To bounce away from him. But my big, heavy body wouldn't budge.

The judge raised a metal tool that looked like a giant cheese scraper. He pressed it against my bulging chest—and pulled.

Pain shot down my chest.

The judge pulled off a long strip of my skin. He held it up to the light, and the judges all studied it.

"Too thin," one of them said.

"Reject," another judge muttered.

My enormous body throbbed and ached with pain. Suddenly I was being shoved across the stage and hoisted onto a wide floor scale.

My body bobbed heavily on the scale. I tried to read my weight. But I couldn't see below my round belly.

"Two hundred pounds!" the judge called out.

"Puny!" a man in the crowd shouted.

"Too small! Throw it back!" another man cried.

The crowd began to chant, "Loser! Loser! Loser!"

"Wait! Check out his hands!" I saw MacColley run up to the front of the stage. "Maybe his hands are worth saving!" he shouted.

Oh no, I thought. I pictured the hands floating in the big jars—and my huge blob of a body started to shake.

"Loser! Loser! Loser!" The jeers and boos rang in my ears.

I saw Pete hoisted up off the stage by a chain hanging from the ceiling. And then I felt a harness slip around my own enormous, round body. I was hoisted off the floor and carried high in the air, toward a door at the side wall.

"Loser! Loser! Loser!" were the last words I heard before disappearing through another dark tunnel.

I followed Pete onto a long conveyor belt. We were flat on our backs. The belt moved quickly.

It was carrying us toward a giant stamping machine pounding down from above. *Stamp. Stamp. Stamp.* The letters on it were backward, but I could read them easily: LOSER.

I took a deep breath. Gathered all my strength. And tried to roll off the conveyor belt.

Grunting and groaning, I strained every muscle. But I couldn't move. I was just too heavy.

"Yeeeooooow!" Pete let out a wail of pain as the giant metal stamp pounded down on him.

Then the big stamper lifted, ready to pound its next victim—me.

As the belt pulled me under it, I shut my eyes and held my breath.

STAMP.

Pain jolted my body. I saw bright red. And then a deep, deep endless black.

≈

A sharp smell awoke me. A sick, putrid odor. Wet and foul. Like rotting vegetables.

I raised my head and stared up at the night sky. A pale half-moon floated behind wisps of cloud.

How long have I been knocked out? I wondered.

"Oooh, the smell," Pete groaned, beside me. "It stinks so bad."

Holding my breath, I gazed around. We were sprawled in some garbage Dumpster. We were lying on top of vegetables. Rotting cabbages. Broken squashes. Decaying melons crawling with flies. Disgusting, putrid pumpkins.

The losers. The rejects.

And now Pete and I were part of the pile.

"Hey—we're smaller," I said. "We're our own size."

"Yeah. We're not blobs anymore!" Pete cried.

My stomach itched violently. I pulled a rotting lettuce from under my shirt. Insects swarmed over it, swarmed over my stomach, my T-shirt.

Pete pulled sticky, wet pumpkin meat from his hair. "I . . . I'm going to be sick," he said.

"Let's get out of here," I said. "We've got to tell someone what's going on in the Youth Building. We've got to warn people."

"We should tell the police," Pete said. "They can't do that to kids! Hurry. Let's find a cop, Colin!"

Holding on to the Dumpster wall, we pulled ourselves to our feet. Our shoes sank in the rotting vegetables. We slid down to our waists. But we managed to grab the top of the Dumpster and hoist ourselves out.

The lights had been turned on. The Ferris wheel whirled behind us. In the outdoor theater a country-music band was tuning up.

"We can find a cop at the front gate," Pete said. "Let's go."

We both took off, running. But we stopped when we heard a voice calling our names. We turned and saw Franny striding up to us, hands on her waist.

"Where did you go?" she asked. "I've been waiting for you."

"You—you won't believe what happened to us!" I cried breathlessly. "It was horrible. We—we've got to find a cop. We've—"

"They're doing horrible things to kids in the Youth Building," Pete said.

"The *what?*" Franny asked. "What Youth Building?"

"It's right back there," I said. I turned and pointed. But there was nothing to point to. An empty patch of grass.

"It was right there. I *know* it was," I insisted.

"I saw you two go into the Fun House," Franny said. "But then I didn't see you come out."

I gaped at her. "Huh? The Fun House?"

She motioned to a brightly lighted building behind us. Giant ghosts and skeletons were painted on the walls. The blinking sign read: HOUSE OF A THOUSAND SCREAMS.

"I saw you two go in, so I waited right here," Franny said. "Did you come out a back door?"

Pete and I stared at each other. "You—you really saw us go in there?" Pete asked Franny.

Franny nodded. "How was it? Was that *you* I heard screaming your heads off in there?"

≈

I didn't understand what had happened to Pete and me. But I didn't want to think about it now. I was happy to return home a half hour later.

"How was it?" Mom asked from the den.

"Okay," I said. "You know. The usual."

"It's late," she called. "Go take a bath and go to bed."

I made my way upstairs and started the bathwater. Then I hurried to my room and started to undress.

Maybe Pete and I *were* in the Fun House the whole time, I thought. Franny wouldn't lie. She saw us.

Maybe we hit our heads or something in there and imagined the whole judging thing.

I tugged off my socks and tossed them on the floor.

I'm just going to put it out of my mind, I decided. I'm going to forget about it and never think about it again.

I pulled off my T-shirt and threw it on the bed. And glimpsed myself in the dresser mirror.

And realized that I *couldn't* forget about what happened.

I *couldn't* pretend it never happened. I *couldn't* ever put it out of my mind.

Because across my chest was a word in big black letters: **LOSER**.

Can You Draw Me?

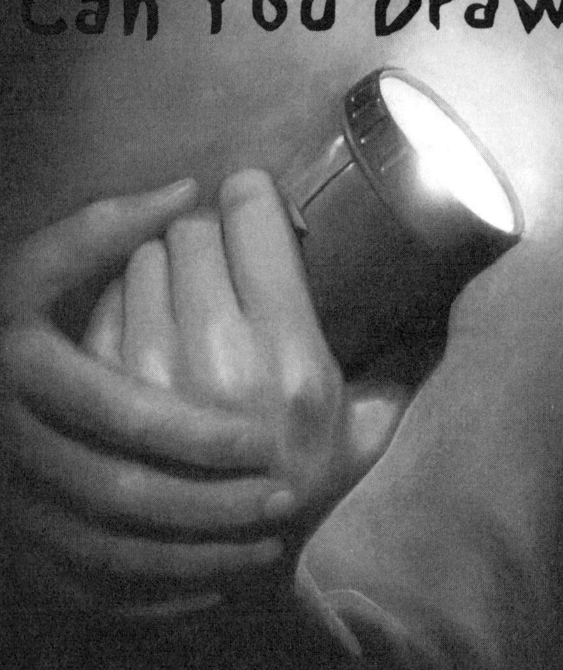

INTRODUCTION

Did you ever wonder why some people can draw and others can't? What kind of strange magic is involved?

When I was a kid, I dreamed of being a cartoonist. I spent hours and hours drawing little comic books. Then one day I looked around and saw that my drawings were like baby scribbles compared to those of the other kids in my class.

I decided I'd better *write* instead of draw. But I've been fascinated by artists ever since.

When I sat down to write this story, I asked myself these questions: What if an artist suddenly lost control of his painting? What if his hand started painting on its own? What if he couldn't control it at all?

How terrifying would that be?

You decide. . . .

ILLUSTRATED BY BLEU TURRELL

I put my brush to the paper and drew the outline of Julie's face. Then I added a few brushstrokes to start her hair. "Hold still," I said. "You can't move until I get the basic lines in."

She giggled. "Dylan, you look so serious."

I could feel myself blushing. The truth is, I had a major crush on Julie. And I wanted this painting to be awesomely good. I really wanted to impress her.

She leaned back on the edge of my bed, her hands behind her pressed on the quilt. Her blond hair was pulled back in a loose ponytail. She wore a blue turtleneck sweater over faded straight-legged jeans.

The late-afternoon sun poured through my bedroom window, spreading a warm, orange glow over the room. Julie kept a smile frozen on her face, which made two big dimples appear on her cheeks.

"How did you get interested in painting?" she asked.

I leaned over my drawing board and started to outline her eyes. "You won't believe it," I said, "but I saw one of those ads in the local newspaper. It had a girl's face in it. And it said: 'Can you draw me?'"

The brush slipped, and I accidentally dabbed a smudge of black paint over her left eye. I'd just gotten these brushes, and I wasn't used to them.

"It was some kind of contest," I continued. "I sent my drawing in—and I won. I won art lessons with this old guy who lives downtown. MacKenzie Douglas. He used to be a very famous magazine illustrator."

"Was he a good teacher?" Julie asked.

"The best!" I said. "I don't know how he did it. But ever since those lessons, I can draw anybody—no problem."

"Cool," Julie said. She stretched her arms. "Are you almost finished? I can't wait to see it."

Before I could answer, I heard heavy, thudding footsteps—and Flash came waddling into the room. The big chimpanzee uttered a few *hoo hoo hoo*'s then jumped into Julie's lap.

Julie let out a startled cry and fell off the bed with the chimp on top of her.

"Mandy!" I yelled for my little sister. She instantly appeared in the doorway. "Mandy—you're supposed to be watching Flash," I said angrily. "How come he got away from you?"

"Because he's a chimp, that's why!" Mandy always has a smart answer for everything.

Julie shoved the chattering chimp off and struggled to her feet. "He's heavy!"

Mandy tugged Flash back to her room. "I'm sorry," I said. "Are you okay? Dad is always bringing pets home from the animal hospital where he works. Flash is a total pest."

"He's kind of cute," Julie said, brushing chimp fur off her sweater. She returned to her perch on the bed. "He just surprised me, that's all."

Just my luck. I try to impress a girl, and a chimpanzee knocks her to the floor.

"Dad brought two macaws home yesterday," I said. "Hear them? They're down in the living room, screeching their heads off. We even had a little pig running around the house last week!"

Julie laughed. "You live in a zoo!"

I leaned over the drawing board and concentrated on the painting. I carefully sketched in the mouth. Julie was the coolest girl in my seventh-grade class. I couldn't believe it when she agreed to pose for me. I knew I had to make this my best portrait ever.

I changed the eyes. I wasn't happy with them. Then I carefully sketched the nose. I worked quickly. The new brush glided easily over the paper.

"How much longer?" Julie asked.

"Not much," I said. "I'm filling in some details."

"Does it really look like me?" she asked.

"You'll see," I replied.

And then my hand made a sharp movement across the page. Whoa, I thought. Why did I do that?

I dipped the brush into the jar of paint. I wanted to fill in the hair. But my hand guided the brush to the mouth. I made several sharp strokes.

"Hey!" I cried out.

"What's wrong?" Julie asked.

"Nothing," I said. But something was terribly wrong.

My hand—it was moving on its own!

The brush painted in lines over Julie's cheeks and forehead. Then it moved to her mouth and began drawing furiously.

I grabbed my hand and tried to pull it away from the page. But it wouldn't budge.

This is *crazy!* I thought. This can't be happening.

My hand is drawing without me!

I have no control. No control at all!

A wave of panic made my whole body shudder. I struggled to control the brush, but it kept moving over the page.

I could feel cold sweat rolling down my forehead. This is terrifying! What is happening to me?

Suddenly Julie jumped up and crossed the room. "Let me see it!" she said. "I can't wait any longer."

"No!" I shouted. "It—it isn't ready!"

"I don't care," she replied, grinning at me. "Let me see this masterpiece!"

I tried to cover it with my body, but Julie grabbed the painting off the drawing board and turned it around to look at it.

"DYLAN!" she screamed. "It's so gross! *Why did you do this?*"

She held the paper between her hands. In the painting her forehead and cheeks were covered with deep, open scars. And a hairy bucktoothed rat poked out of her open mouth.

"I—I—I didn't!" I sputtered.

She let out a furious cry and ripped the painting in half. "You're not funny," she cried angrily. "You're not funny. You're just gross." Then she stormed out of the room.

"But Julie—" I called.

A few seconds later I heard the front door slam behind her.

"How did that happen?" I asked out loud in a trembling voice. "How?" I stared at my hand, as if it could answer.

≈

I barely ate any dinner. I told Mom and Dad I wasn't feeling well. Up in my room I couldn't concentrate on my homework.

I kept thinking about my painting of Julie with the rat poking out of her mouth. I couldn't stop thinking about how my hand had moved, out of my control, ruining the painting.

I went to bed early, but I couldn't sleep.

A little after midnight I climbed out of bed and turned on the ceiling light. Then I made my way to the drawing table.

I had to prove to myself that I could still paint. I had to prove that I wasn't going crazy or something.

I set up a mirror on my drawing table. Then I put a fresh sheet of paper down and picked up one of my new brushes.

I dipped the brush into a fresh jar of paint and began to draw myself. My eyes moved from the mirror to the drawing. I started with the eyes this time. Then I sketched in my snubby nose and my full mouth.

So far, so good, I thought.

I moved to the hair. My hair is not easy to draw because it's short and spiky and shoots out in a million directions.

But the brush glided quickly. My hand felt sure and steady.

Yesss! I thought.

But I celebrated too early.

I dipped my brush into the paint again and lowered it to outline my face. I started on the chin—but my hand jerked to the side.

I stared in horror as it began drawing on its own. Drawing something where my neck should be.

"NO!" I screamed. I tugged with all my strength. But my other hand moved with incredible force.

I could only stand and watch it move around the paper. The hand was out of my control. Moving on its own!

"NOOOOOO!" A scream burst from my throat.

The bedroom door flew open. Mom and Dad came running in in their pajamas, their hair tousled, their faces sleepy. "Dylan—what's wrong?" they both cried.

Dad grabbed my painting from the table. They both stared at it.

It showed me with a noose around my neck. My tongue was hanging out, and my eyes were bulging.

"Why did you paint this?" Dad demanded. "What are you doing up so late?"

"I—I don't know," I replied.

"Why did you paint such a sick thing?" Mom asked. "Is something troubling you, Dylan? Something you want to talk about?"

"I—I don't know," I repeated.

≈

I stayed away from my drawing table for the rest of the week. I hid the paint jars and brushes in the closet.

I didn't want to think about what had happened. Every time I pictured my hand moving on its own, I wanted to scream in horror.

On Monday I had no choice. I had to bring my paintbrushes to school. Mr. Vella, the art teacher, had chosen me and four other kids to paint a mural on the long art-room wall.

When I passed Julie in the hall, she looked the other way. I saw kids grinning at me. I guessed that Julie had told them what had happened.

I hurried to the art room. Kids were at their tables, waiting to watch us five artists go to work. "Remember, people, the theme of the mural is *America the Beautiful*," Mr. Vella said.

He guided me to the end of the long wall. "I saved this square for you, Dylan," he said. "From here to the window. I see you brought your own brushes. What are you going to paint?"

I gazed at the blank white canvas. "A farm scene, I think," I answered. "Some animals. Maybe a farm family."

"Sounds good," Mr. Vella said. "Go to work." He moved on to the next artist, an eighth-grade girl named Willa Myers.

I glanced down the line and realized I was the only seventh grader. I'd better do a really good job, I thought.

I started with a pencil. I sketched several sheep, a cow, some horses poking their heads over a fence. I sketched a farmhouse in the background. A family of four bent over, feeding seed to a bunch of chickens.

Mr. Vella moved up and down the row of artists, making comments and suggestions. "That looks very good, Dylan," he said, helping to finish my pencil sketch of the chickens. "You can begin to paint now."

I carried paint jars over to my spot. Then I prepared my paintbrushes.

My hand moved too quickly. The brush swept over my pencil sketch. I tried to control the brushstrokes. But once again my hand took off.

No—please! Please don't do this! I silently begged.

But I couldn't stop my hand.

I tried to drop the brush. But my fingers held tight. The brush kept moving up and down, drawing without me. Drawing on its own.

Am I going crazy?

"Dylan—what are you doing?" I heard Mr. Vella's alarmed cry from down the row. And I heard kids laughing.

My hand finished the farm family. The four people were bending over, headless. Blood poured from their open necks. Their heads were on the ground, being pecked apart by the chickens.

The cow and horses were vomiting. Piles of puke were puddled around their feet. The sheep had bullet holes in their sides.

"Dylan! I want you to stop this right now!" Mr. Vella shouted.

"I—I CAN'T STOP!" I shouted.

The kids erupted in laughter. They thought I was joking.

"HELP ME! MR. VELLA—HELP ME!"

My hand pulled me to the side. I bumped into Willa Myers and kicked over her paint jars.

My brush attacked her drawing. I scrawled thick black lines over the city scene she had started. My hand scribbled and jabbed.

"Dylan—get away!" Willa cried.

"I can't!" I shouted. "I can't stop it!"

My brush jabbed at Willa's face. I painted black smudges on her cheeks, then a zigzag line across her hair.

She shrieked and staggered back.

"HELP ME! SOMEBODY!" I wailed.

The class had grown silent now.

My brush dipped into a red-paint jar. And I began scrawling ugly faces on the wall. On the floor. I swung away from the canvas and began to paint red bars on the window.

"STOP ME! STOP ME!" The cry burst from my throat. The hand was jerking me one way, then the other. Painting. Painting. I couldn't stop it. "HELP ME!"

Mr. Vella rushed over. "Dylan—what's wrong? Get a grip on yourself. I—"

My hand painted a thick red stripe down the center of his face. Then a stripe down the front of his sweater.

With a sputtering cry he grabbed my shoulders. I spun away from him, and my brush swiped down the sleeve of his sweater. He was covered in red paint. Then my hand moved to the art-room door and began painting the door.

"I CAN'T STOP! CAN'T STOP!" I shrieked. "CAN'T ANY-BODY HELP ME?"

≈

My parents kept me home the next day. They couldn't decide whether to be angry or worried about me. So they were both.

I stayed in my room. I tried to read my schoolwork, but I just couldn't think straight. The macaws were chattering away down-stairs. I turned on the TV with the sound real loud to drown them out. But I couldn't concentrate on it, either.

I couldn't believe it when Mr. Vella paid a surprise visit after school. My mother showed him to my room. "Dylan is very sorry for what he did," she told the art teacher. Then she went downstairs and left us alone.

Mr. Vella sat down at my desk. "How are you feeling today?" he asked.

"Okay," I replied. I apologized for what had happened in class. "I . . . can't really explain it," I said. I sat on the edge of my bed.

He studied me for a long while. "How long have you been interested in painting?" he asked finally.

"I didn't really get interested in it until I won some lessons. From an artist named MacKenzie Douglas."

Mr. Vella squinted at me. "MacKenzie Douglas? I read in the paper that he died three weeks ago."

I gasped. "Really? But I don't understand. I just finished my lessons with him a few weeks ago. And he . . . he sent me some of his brushes last week."

Mr. Vella glanced at the paintbrushes on my drawing table. "Strange . . . " he muttered.

We talked a short while longer. Then Mr. Vella made his way to the door. "I just wanted to make sure you are okay," he said. "That was frightening yesterday."

"I think I'm all right," I said. "I'll definitely be back in school tomorrow."

He gave me a wave and headed downstairs. I could hear him talking with my mom.

I stepped up to the drawing table and studied the paintbrushes. I felt bad that MacKenzie Douglas had died.

I picked up the long-handled brushes one by one. When did he send them? I wondered. How did they reach me two weeks after he died?

That night I fell asleep quickly. I dreamed I was painting the sky. I wanted to paint white, fluffy clouds. But I couldn't reach high enough.

I was awakened by a scraping sound. "Huh? Who's there?" I whispered.

Blinking myself awake, I raised my head from the pillow. I squinted into the dim light—and gasped.

The paintbrushes were floating in the air.

They scraped across the paper on the drawing table. Tilting, bobbing, sliding up and down—the brushes were painting.

Painting without me!

"NO!" With a terrified cry, I leaped out of bed. I lurched across the room and made a grab for the brushes.

The brushes jerked and jabbed the air. I wrapped my hands around the handles and struggled to hold on to them.

My hands were pulled above my head. The brushes twirled and jerked, as if trying to escape. But I tightened my grip and held on.

I've got to get rid of them, I decided. I've got to get them out of this house. If I do, my life will go back to normal.

Squeezing the brush handles tightly, I crept downstairs. I made my way to the kitchen and stepped out the back door.

The ground was hard and cold under my bare feet. A chilling wind fluttered my pajamas. I ran across the wet grass to the back of the garage.

Four metal trash cans stood along the garage wall. I lifted the lid on the first can and tossed the brushes in. Then I slammed down the lid and made sure it was on tight.

Shivering, I ran back into the house. I climbed into bed and pulled the covers up to my chin. I could sleep easily now. I thought I had won a big victory.

I didn't know that my brush troubles weren't over yet.

≈

The next morning I peered through my bedroom window down

to the backyard. "What?" I let out a hoarse cry when I saw that the first trash can had been tipped over.

I turned and saw the paintbrushes stacked on the side of my drawing table. "Oh no!" I moaned. "They're back!"

My heart pounding, I raced across the room and grabbed them. My parents were in the backyard talking to our neighbors. Holding the brushes tightly in both hands, I ran down the stairs to the basement.

I carried them past the laundry room to Dad's workshop. My dad is a real handyman, and he has a lot of major-league tools.

I flicked the switch on Dad's table saw. Of course, I'm not allowed to use it. But this was an emergency.

The saw hummed to life. The round, jagged blade began to spin. Holding the ends of the brushes, I slid them toward the blade.

"Good-bye, brushes!" I shouted.

The big blade made a whining sound as it grated against the first wooden brush handle.

To my shock the wood didn't split. The brush bounced off. The blade couldn't cut through it!

I tried again, pushing the brush handle against the whirring blade. The blade whined—and bent. The brush bounced off, unharmed.

No. This is impossible, I thought. This can't be happening.

I shut off the table saw. I grabbed the blowtorch from the floor beside the worktable.

I *definitely* was not allowed to use this. But I didn't care. I was in a total panic. I had to destroy these brushes—before they ruined my life!

I set the brushes on the concrete floor. Then I lit the blowtorch. A bright-blue flame burst out with a roar.

"Yikes!"

Startled, I nearly dropped the heavy thing onto the floor. But I held on and aimed the flame at the brushes.

And waited for them to burn. And waited.

The brushes didn't burn.

Cold panic swept over me. I stared at the brushes lying unharmed under the powerful, hot flame.

I'll take them far away, I thought. Maybe I can mail them to another country. Or maybe I can bury them.

I turned off the blowtorch. Then I gathered up the brushes and carried them back to my room.

I tried to drop them onto my drawing table, but the brushes stuck to my hands.

I struggled to uncurl my fingers, to let the brushes fall. But instead my fingers tightened around the handles.

"No! No! No!" I chanted, squirming, pulling, twisting, fighting the power of the brushes.

But I no longer had control of my hands. They were dipping the brushes into paint, then moving to the paper on the drawing board.

"No! No! No!"

I couldn't stop them. I couldn't free myself from them.

The brushes scraped across the paper, painting words in fat red letters.

"No! No!"

I gaped in horror at the message the brushes had written:

YOUR HANDS ARE MINE NOW. WE WILL PAINT TOGETHER—FOREVER.

The message done, the paintbrushes dropped from my hands beside the paper.

I was gasping for breath. My entire body trembled. I stared down at them. How can I get rid of these brushes? *How?*

Then, suddenly, I had an idea.

≈

A month later Julie and I were a
magazine show on TV in her den. Juli
make popcorn, but I pulled her back
"Watch."

She sat back down, and we watc
show. The camera backed up, and we
hand. The chimp was all dressed up i

Dad led Flash to a drawing tabl
long-handled brush, and started to p

"This is amazing!" the TV report
monster. His paintings are strange a
better than most humans!"

The camera caught a big smile o
selling Flash's work to museums all

The camera moved in close o
changed brushes and continued to pa

"How did this happen?" the repo
discover this chimp had so much tal

Dad smiled into the camera. "It
"My son Dylan gave Flash an extra se
in front of a drawing board—and the

Flash jumped up and down and
moved the brushes over the paper.

Julie turned to me. "Dylan, d
"You're so serious about your paintin
is such a famous artist?"

A big smile spread over my fa
way!" And I settled back to watch F

to the backyard. "What?" I let out a hoarse cry when I saw that the first trash can had been tipped over.

I turned and saw the paintbrushes stacked on the side of my drawing table. "Oh no!" I moaned. "They're back!"

My heart pounding, I raced across the room and grabbed them. My parents were in the backyard talking to our neighbors. Holding the brushes tightly in both hands, I ran down the stairs to the basement.

I carried them past the laundry room to Dad's workshop. My dad is a real handyman, and he has a lot of major-league tools.

I flicked the switch on Dad's table saw. Of course, I'm not allowed to use it. But this was an emergency.

The saw hummed to life. The round, jagged blade began to spin. Holding the ends of the brushes, I slid them toward the blade.

"Good-bye, brushes!" I shouted.

The big blade made a whining sound as it grated against the first wooden brush handle.

To my shock the wood didn't split. The brush bounced off. The blade couldn't cut through it!

I tried again, pushing the brush handle against the whirring blade. The blade whined—and bent. The brush bounced off, unharmed.

No. This is impossible, I thought. This can't be happening.

I shut off the table saw. I grabbed the blowtorch from the floor beside the worktable.

I *definitely* was not allowed to use this. But I didn't care. I was in a total panic. I had to destroy these brushes—before they ruined my life!

I set the brushes on the concrete floor. Then I lit the blowtorch. A bright-blue flame burst out with a roar.

"Yikes!"

Startled, I nearly dropped the heavy thing onto the floor. But I held on and aimed the flame at the brushes.

And waited for them to burn. And waited.

The brushes didn't burn.

Cold panic swept over me. I stared at the brushes lying unharmed under the powerful, hot flame.

I'll take them far away, I thought. Maybe I can mail them to another country. Or maybe I can bury them.

I turned off the blowtorch. Then I gathered up the brushes and carried them back to my room.

I tried to drop them onto my drawing table, but the brushes stuck to my hands.

I struggled to uncurl my fingers, to let the brushes fall. But instead my fingers tightened around the handles.

"No! No! No!" I chanted, squirming, pulling, twisting, fighting the power of the brushes.

But I no longer had control of my hands. They were dipping the brushes into paint, then moving to the paper on the drawing board.

"No! No! No!"

I couldn't stop them. I couldn't free myself from them.

The brushes scraped across the paper, painting words in fat red letters.

"No! No!"

I gaped in horror at the message the brushes had written:

YOUR HANDS ARE MINE NOW. WE WILL PAINT TOGETHER—FOREVER.

The message done, the paintbrushes dropped from my hands beside the paper.

I was gasping for breath. My entire body trembled. I stared down at them. How can I get rid of these brushes? *How?*

Then, suddenly, I had an idea.

≈

A month later Julie and I were at her house, watching a newsmagazine show on TV in her den. Julie started toward the kitchen to make popcorn, but I pulled her back. "It's coming on now," I said. "Watch."

She sat back down, and we watched my dad appear on the TV show. The camera backed up, and we could see Flash holding Dad's hand. The chimp was all dressed up in a silvery suit.

Dad led Flash to a drawing table. Flash sat down, picked up a long-handled brush, and started to paint.

"This is amazing!" the TV reporter exclaimed. "He's painting a monster. His paintings are strange and ugly. But this chimp paints better than most humans!"

The camera caught a big smile on Dad's face. "That's why we're selling Flash's work to museums all over the world," he said.

The camera moved in close on Flash's hands as the chimp changed brushes and continued to paint.

"How did this happen?" the reporter asked Dad. "How did you discover this chimp had so much talent?"

Dad smiled into the camera. "It was an accident, really," he said. "My son Dylan gave Flash an extra set of brushes. We sat Flash down in front of a drawing board—and the rest is history!"

Flash jumped up and down and uttered a *hoo hoo hoo* as his hands moved the brushes over the paper.

Julie turned to me. "Dylan, don't you feel bad?" she asked. "You're so serious about your painting. Aren't you jealous that Flash is such a famous artist?"

A big smile spread over my face. "Me? Jealous?" I said. "No way!" And I settled back to watch Flash paint.